Najat El Hachmi was born in Nador in the Rif Valley in Morocco in 1979, by which time her father had already emigrated to Catalonia where Najat went to live at the age of eight when the family came together again. She has a degree in Arabic Philology from the University of Barcelona. Her first novel, *The Last Patriarch*, won the Ramon Llull Catalan national prize for literature in 2008. It has been translated into ten languages, was on the shortlist for the Prix Méditerranée Étranger and won the Prix Ulysse.

Praise for *The Last Patriarch*

'El Hachmi's searing *Bildungsroman* boldly mixes family and cultural history, feminist polemic and satirical humour, and won Catalonia's prestigious Ramon Llull prize... The undercurrent of menace in the complicated relationship between father and daughter is leavened by the buoyancy of the translation and El Hachmi's light, conversational writing; the ending is truly transgressive' Catherine Taylor, *Guardian*

'An exciting fictional take on politics and the family' Melissa Katsoulis, *Sunday Telegraph*

El Hachmi excels in her portrayal... never simplistic about oppression... *The Last Patriarch* works on all its levels: a document of the changes assailing modern Morocco; a story of the suffering and success of migration; and a feminist diatribe on how desire and courage can defeat patriarchal values. Najat El Hachmi's narrative poise, humour and fresh, unrepressed language turn her painful subject matter into a pleasure to read' Michael Eaude, *Independent*

'A lively depiction of family life in Morocco and Catalonia' *Stylist*

The Body Hunter

Najat El Hachmi

Translated from the Catalan by Peter Bush

The translation of this work was supported by a grant from
the Institut Ramon Llull

A complete catalogue record for this book can be obtained from
the British Library on request

First published in 2011 as *La caçadora de cossos* by
Columna Edicions, S.A. Barcelona

First published in this translation in 2013 by Serpent's Tail,
an imprint of Profile Books Ltd
3A Exmouth House
Pine Street
London EC1R 0JH
www.serpentstail.com

ISBN 978 1 84668 901 7
eISBN 978 1 84765 858 6

Designed and typeset by sue@lambledesign.demon.co.uk
Printed and bound by CPI Group (UK) Ltd, Croydon, CR0 4YY

10 9 8 7 6 5 4 3 2 1

For Carlos

The city simultaneously prompts mixo*philia* as much as mixo*phobia*.

ZYGMUNT BAUMAN, *City of Fears, City of Hopes*

I am but the hand you use to touch.

GABRIEL FERRATER

I want my half orange, but I'll eat mandarins as I go.

Written on a blackboard in a Gràcia hairdressers

She's standing opposite a door at the top of steps that are far too steep. And hesitating. She's not rung the bell yet. She wipes the sweat – or nervous tremor – off her cheek with the back of her hand, a caress almost. Though, of course, it isn't a caress; they explore slower, more tentative paths across your skin. She looks over her shoulder: one day somebody decided to build those narrow steps rising in hot pursuit of each other and created a precipitous staircase. What's more, no banister. Beautiful marble steps from another era that make you dizzy. How stupid to stand there, not daring to ring, like a little kid. Hardly, kids are bolder because they know less, and haven't a clue what might be lurking behind the door. What if a neighbour saw her? It's only a job like any other, a way to pay the bills. What's wrong with topping up your earnings? True, she'd pledged never to do this kind of domestic work, but she'd been obsessed by the prospect from the moment a friend at the factory suggested it. She has wiped her forehead, wiped her sweaty hands over the stitching on her trousers, switched her bag hand a couple of times, scratched her right ear until it's sore, and now she has run out of excuses, she feels frightened when she rings the bell and sets off that strident buzz.

THE COLLECTION

Mr Ethereal

Sir, if you could only see my memories of all those men, though I always told myself it was about having a good time, putting a bit of spice into life. I've never managed to forget a single one, however briefly they lasted.

I remember Mr Ethereal. Mr Ethereal was a young guy. Yes, I'd say he was still very much a young guy, who would walk up a slope close to where I lived. We walked up that slope together a lot. Until I realized we were heading to the same place, where I was going to clean and he went to loaf around. Right now I couldn't tell you what attracted me so much that I stuck with him for so long. But it wasn't all the time, was more off than on, and never a real relationship. What's a relationship anyway? Where do you start? I don't have a serious girlfriend, he told me, just the casual sort. I didn't ask him what he meant by his girlfriends, or what he thought that meant, or whether they were half serious, I mean, that he simply went to bed with them whenever he felt like it. When you think people haven't left you anything to remember them by, you keep quiet about such things. I was saying that I don't know what attracted me to Mr Ethereal, maybe it was his bottomless eyes, or the expression permanently fixed on his face as if someone had pressed the pause button. He took ages to answer questions people usually answered without a second thought. When it was all over, that bothered me a lot.

Mr Ethereal invited me to lunch at his place and we both knew where *that* would end but it took longer than I imagined. Sure it was great sitting on his balcony warming up a bit in the February sun and swapping our life stories, drinking tea to which he wouldn't let me add sugar because he'd flavoured it with anisette and anisette is sweet enough. Every sip left a nasty, warm, bland taste in my mouth. We found our lives had things in common. We'd both been reasonably happy kids in reasonably conventional families; we'd not stood out either way from our classmates and had decided to give up studying because we'd no clear idea where we wanted to go. When we'd established the common elements in our past lives we felt on a high and that smoothed the way for what came later. As if it was fated. In fact, we could have shared those things with almost anybody. Looking back, it seems clear we hardly mentioned how our lines began to diverge at that point in the conversation when he told me he'd left for Canada at the age of eighteen and I hadn't dared reveal that I'd hardly been outside my city. Or when he talked about how he'd gone back to studying after a sabbatical year when he'd learned how to cure broken bodies. Studies that obviously cost a mint and made him what he was now.

I ignored these differences, just as I didn't go along with that universal rule hammered home by every film and television series that says you must never, on any account, fuck a guy on your first date. I was thinking about all that, the scenes of sloppy kisses and girls going upstairs by themselves, shutting doors in forlorn faces, when I felt something press hard on my belly button. Something hard coming from behind the knee up to my bum. And this was before he'd even kissed me or we'd passionately embraced, him making the first touch, even before we'd rolled around on the kitchen floor. Not that we ever did do it on any kitchen floor. I'd say I was won over by the bold, hard way he pushed me onto the bed, and that other slow, suggestive movement I found strangely invasive and arousing. He never did it again. I sometimes thought it was just a ploy, a trick he'd worked on, knowing full well the effect it would have on my body. Because Mr Ethereal knew a lot about bodies, even if he knew next to nothing about anything else. He studied and investigated them, knew the names of every muscle, limb and joint. That was why he grabbed a soft drink bottle when we first went to bed and pressed on a muscle that connected with another I didn't even know existed. I made sure I gripped the table tight to ensure his pressure on my flesh lasted longer.

In fact, sex with Mr Ethereal was perfect. He slid and hid himself in my body, then resurfaced powerfully. He acted with a deceptive, gentle tenderness and then abruptly turned into a dominator. How *do* they know I love to be dominated? I never tell them, they just know. But, I have to say, Mr Ethereal was a courteous, subtle dominator and used tricks others would have never tried to get me to play my favourite role. Like the sudden, energetic way he'd pull my arms away from his body and force them down against the pillow, leaving me helpless, or slid his fingers down my back until they were inside me without my even noticing, then sticking it into me without hurting. When I think back now, I must be honest and say that sex with him was really perfect. Mr Ethereal was a body tamer. He never started off rough or crude, he was into rhythm, the most difficult thing for a lover, but then I'd start to think it was all one big joke. I'd burst out laughing when I saw him looking so serious from on high, as if his eyes were going all dark. That's right, those blue glassy eyes of his changed with the really serious orgasms he usually had, as if it were the climax to a tragedy. Maybe I just got bored, bored of sex transforming his face into something so grotesque, or of him making it out to be such a big deal or saying so little it exasperated me. These are things you don't see when desire is driving you on, as if you were in a race and all that mattered was reaching the tape. You only see the kind of thing that worried me afterwards when you are quiet and relaxed, and, in any case, I'd only start sprinting when I saw desire flash in a man's eyes.

When did I begin to turn against him? Turn against him, hate him to the point of repulsion, not want to be near him. I could tolerate him, but only at a distance, when I couldn't smell him. When exactly did I stop racing in tandem with him? Because, for sure, he hadn't changed, he was the same as at the start, but I'd stopped seeing him with the same eyes. I'm good at deceiving myself when I feel the need for a body, I tell myself it's pleasure and no more, but I can't deceive myself for long. Fortunately or not, who can say, such self-deception is short-lived. That's how I began to think about the things that bugged me about him: when he was frantically licking me in the hope of a reaction and I could only think about how slow-paced he was when he wasn't fucking, about the despair on his face when he couldn't light the burner on the cooker, how he got upset when it was late and he had to walk along the dark streets that go from my house to his. Sure he was only young but he was old enough not to be afraid of the dark. Or what about when he didn't eat salad at a party because the lettuce leaves had been in contact with tuna and he never ate meat. When he is licking me, hoping I'm going to come at any moment, I think about how he counts his almonds and rations them over a number of days so they last longer. I make an effort to cover my nose to keep out his smell that used to be so pleasant. I don't come anymore because I don't relate him to sex now and I don't know if I do that for myself or as an act of revenge because he is the pits and yet still part of me. Until I say stop, leave off, and he says, no, I can't, I don't want to leave you halfway and I say I don't feel like it, I'm alright, and now it's all about eluding the pleasure he wants to impose on me. He doesn't get it, but he doesn't get annoyed because he's long since passed the halfway mark.

Then he became crazy about entering me from behind, something I liked as a bonus, but after one session in particular he always wanted to end up in that same place. We'd kiss and embrace but when I wasn't watching he'd stick it in there, as if he was obsessed with the back entrance. A lot of men are like that, when they do something with you they've never done with another woman, it soon becomes what they always want. And if you are cheeky enough to say that what you like one day, you don't necessarily want the day after, though maybe the day after that, fine, they look at you all upset as if you'd gone mad. But the way Mr Ethereal went after me was rather animal-like and he reminded me of dogs when they sniff each other the moment they meet. He'd said he'd never dared do it like that before he'd been with me, but I thought it was because it was taboo or unusual, or he was afraid I'd suck him off in front until he disappeared completely. Or was that when I was afraid of sucking off the men I was fucking? As I don't like thinking about such things, I did all I could to get him to change his ways, silently guided him, made sure I didn't turn my back on him, but in the end I was bored because he always seemed irritated, became dull and deadpan and all our sex was a big letdown. I thought he was trying some kind of blackmail, for when I said no not like that he'd go all limp in bed leaving me to do the work. As if he was saying, 'If we can't do that, you just do what you want.'

I also took against him because he talked about other women's bodies. I never said anything to him, naturally, because right from the start it had been made clear we weren't going steady, that he only had casual girlfriends, but he'd no need to tell me how he was aroused by the sight of the naked bodies of the women who came to see him through his job, because he had to cure them on his bunk bed and there was no way round that. Lucky he was a real professional, he'd say, but he went on talking about his patients who gave him a hard-on when they were on hand. I also think he did it on purpose. He'd always said he didn't want a conventional relationship, that everything should be freer and more flexible.

And that sums up the pair of us: friends who got together to fuck, like so many couples of our age. Except that I was no friend of his before doing it with him the first time and still wasn't after we broke up, even if our sexual encounters had been more frequent than encounters between friends. No need to label things, he'd say, why do we have to be like other couples and kill everything by sticking on labels. No need to. I was fine with that, I wasn't interested in a life-long relationship, those that begin, go through every stage and come to an end. Passion at the start, followed by something like love, then hatred and final indifference. I didn't want to take that route.

But our relationship stopped being entirely open or at least I noticed it was only open for him. I let him know when I wanted him and he would let me know when he wanted to be with me and the two things normally coincided. Until one day he sent me a message saying, 'Can I come?' and I said no. Not that I didn't feel like it but I was in a bar drinking a beer with Him, and He was already caressing a finger of mine and talking non-stop. He was quite the opposite of Mr Ethereal. Tense, always in a rush, plump, short with lots of flesh on Him, not like tall, skinny Mr Ethereal. Right, if I had to define Him, I'd say He was all flesh and I imagined myself disappearing into his flesh. He was also fond of excesses, He'd never have counted his almonds; He'd have scoffed the lot to a chorus of animal grunts. A wild boar. I'd think of wild boars running through woods when He told me how important his work was, wiping the corners of his lips with two fingers more often than was usual, before wiping them under his nose. He ran his hand through his hair, kept shifting the leg resting on the stool by the bar in that shadowy dive where I received that message from Mr Ethereal when I was outside.

Out in the street, stumbling over the flagstones lit by the streetlights, I could hear his desire summoning me as I read the message – 'Can I come?' – that had been on my mobile for three hours – and I replied that he couldn't. 'I can't' at one a.m. is hardly the same as 'I can't' at ten p.m.

The thing died a death of its own accord. Either I was already interested in Him or had become interested in Him by dint of the disenchantment sparked by Mr Ethereal, who always wanted to do it in the rear and talked about other women's bodies because we weren't set to marry, or whatever, but I had turned against him and that stopped me from wanting to go near his body. Especially when he asked me what I was doing awake at one a.m. and I told him I was drinking beer with a friend. But was it a friend, a special friend or just a friend? Hell, a friend, how many meanings does that word have? It was then he said something that stripped off all his masks: don't you know what a man is after when he invites a girl out for a beer? What a pity all round, because in the beginning he was polite, if not poetic, and at the end, he was totally pathetic. Anyone who'd been there would have agreed. I had no choice but to push him out of the door and slam it behind him one day when he came, when you might have assumed we were only good friends and wouldn't get embroiled again because I didn't want to and he was soon mauling me on the sofa and when I said no, he said why not, I can see you are panting for it. No way, I shouted before he began bawling and his cool, calm gestures turned into a grotesque show of crummy violence that made him look a real fool. Hey, get the fuck out of here and don't ever speak to me again. I was forced to use all my body weight to remove the foot he'd stuck between the door and the door frame, and that gave the whole scene the vulgar aftertaste of a B-movie.

Naturally he tried it on time and again, but now I saw him for what he was and he could do nothing to restore his aura as guru and mythical lover. I was kind to him because, though we met up afterwards and chatted like friends, I never told him how I'd got embroiled with a Ghanaian he introduced me to, with whom I'd danced at the tuna salad party when he'd stared at us so edgily. Now I've told you all this, sir, I'd like to know what you think, but I still don't know you well enough, still don't know exactly who you are and you must think I'm mad to reveal this kind of detail to a complete stranger.

the Ghanaian

You'll probably be shocked, sir, if I tell you I've always liked
men who are different. Or maybe not, because you seem like a
man of the world, even though you never move beyond these
four walls. Fascinated would be the right word. Men with
features that distinguish them from the crowd, from the men
I'm familiar with, the usual suspects, drew me like a magnet.
Fairer hair than is common around here, darker skin, longish
arms or glassy eyes, accents not from my city. And then men
from very distant lands began to appear and it was a struggle
to quell the desire to try them all. Now I don't understand why
I was so keen to go after them. I'd walk along the streets where
they lived. They'd stand together on the pavements watching
girls pass by and shouting with every step we took; it would
have been so easy to beckon to one and try him out simply
because he came from a country I'd never visited. Maybe I was
frightened, the same fear that made them seem irresistible,
but fear can also go by the name of mystery. Yes, you might
laugh to hear me say that, but fear and mystery are two sides
of the same coin. That's why I shook off my fears one day, like
a cat making a dash for it, and flipped the coin. That was how
I stopped simply tolerating their stares when I walked past

them, when they rubbed the back of my hand as they gave me a trolley in the supermarket or I felt their breath on the back of my neck when they sat behind me in the cinema. I couldn't tell you if I was the one going after them or if all those *different* guys were chasing me.

Maybe after Mr Ethereal I found it easier to clear the barrier between them and me, as if, in comparison, the men from my city no longer had that shine that made them desirable. Obviously I know there were exceptions. Maybe Mr Ethereal had nothing to do with it and I was simply fed up of living for that world that had sprung up around me in my neighbourhood. Expressed that way, it sounds rather greedy, doesn't it? But I really liked the sight of that all-you-can-eat buffet. My eyes flitted from one dish to the next wanting to taste the lot and I was afraid I wouldn't have room to take a bite from each and every one.

In a practical sense, Mr Ethereal had a lot to do with my meeting the Ghanaian. I don't remember his name, but he was taller and thinner, and the muscles were so taut under his skin you could trace every one. They danced under his lean skin. His fingers seemed never-ending, all of him seemed never-ending. Like an infinite tightrope. I'm sure you'd agree with my description if you could only see him.

I have very vivid memories of what attracted me to the Ghanaian: his skin was dark in a way I'd never seen before, and gave out heat as if it had soaked up the rays of the sun for years. I immediately imagined him under the sun on the savannah in a previous life that had finally led him to my cold world. It really was like that, however absurd and clichéd it might seem.

Skin glowing from within, not on the surface, urging me to go after him. And a very unusual shade of black. No, there's not one colour black, it comes in lots of different shades. Why are there so many words to describe other colours and only one for black? Because, of course, every inch of him was black, but the black of his eyes was different to the black of his eyelids or of his dark curls or the glinting black hair around his sex. No one could pin down those shades of black or describe skin that isn't smooth or thin, I can vouch for that. Not that his skin was hard but it was thicker, as if it was made from some other material. That sounds horrific, right? Like something a real racist might say and not someone in love with every different kind of man, but I can tell you from experience that their skin *has* different thicknesses and textures. Though, come to think of it now, maybe I just wanted them to feel different, so I could say they were different. You make me wonder about that.

We danced together at that party I went to with Mr Ethereal, crotch to crotch. They dance like that, as if they were having sex and I quickly got into that American music that wasn't at all Ghana. I don't know if I did so partly to annoy Mr Ethereal or if I really let myself be swept up by those black bodies surrounding me, so many swaying groins and gleaming smiles entertained by the sight of me trying to dance like them. I didn't realise this, naturally, but not very long after, feeling myself desired by so many men who passed me round and Mr Ethereal, a wallflower, glass in hand, taking it all in, I was out to the world and dripping sweat. The party was being held in a small flat, lots of people, all really huge.

They included the Ghanaian, the one who became *my*

Ghanaian, and he too was different. Thinner, tauter, longer fingers. The music made it hard to understand him and the fact he didn't know our language, but he did manage to ask me my name and tell me his. Almost immediatcly he asked whether Mr Ethereal was my boyfriend, right when we were dancing next to him, and he was looking really upset. No, I shouted, we are just good friends, aren't we? And I smiled at him and grabbed the Ghanaian's shoulders, tossing my head back and letting my whole back bend away from him. The Ghanaian looked surprised because he thought I *had* come with him. No, I hadn't, I said, and he tried to say we should fix a date by ourselves. I agreed but Mr Ethereal grabbed my arm and started moving his pelvis in an absurd imitation of what the others were doing. Poor Mr Ethereal, when I think about it, I gave him a hard time that night. Though we left soon after and I was so intent on finding my coat in a heap of coats I didn't think to say goodbye to the Ghanaian.

And then one day I bumped into him in a square or street and he called after me. And we stood and talked, neither of us really understanding each other very much, but the words were only a background melody, we were more interested in following the movements of the other's lips, as they opened and closed between words, as they made pauses not required by what we were saying. Reactions confirming our desire. I'd already learned how to talk with my lips when there was silence, I left my lips slightly open, the air coming out smelled, blood was rushing there, my nostrils flared the way they do when you are ready for sex. I sometimes bit my cheek, a habit I'd got into that took years to throw off. It was a signal a clever enough lover picked up straightaway.

I told him I was on my way home and he wanted to come with me. We walked up a steep street in my neighbourhood as far as my front door. And it was inevitable, like in the films, inevitable, he'd come in, wouldn't even need inviting, only an open door. But the Ghanaian was wary and couldn't make his mind up about what to do while I was enjoying a whiff of his armpits from the other end of the sofa. The smell of sweaty armpits differs from country to country, no one ever talks about this but it's true. It isn't? Believe me, I know what I'm talking about. It's not about some generating a smell and others not, or some using deodorant and others not, it's not about cleanliness. If I'd a crowd of men lined up after a shower, I could guess where they come from by the smell of their armpits or even the insides of their elbows, and do it blindfold. And the Ghanaian's smell was rich, like plasticine, and went straight to my crotch. That's something else not everyone is aware of, that each kind of sweat hits you in a different place.

In the end, he didn't have much to say for himself, he couldn't find any more to say about his brothers and sisters in Africa or about the one who lived in the United States and was married to an American woman who took in orphans. Our words dried up. He acted as if I'd something on my face he had to remove in a gesture that seemed ages old, from a bygone era. Maybe his long fingers that were too big for my face made me think that or maybe they just caressed clumsily. In all that time I never found out whether it was them or where they'd come from. For whatever reason, the Ghanaian hadn't a clue when it came to caressing, but the moment I started crushing his never-ending lips, I forgot all about his caresses. His thick, fleshy lips were a dream. The Ghanaian's lips could have been enough to satisfy me. Telling him I just wanted him so I could kiss them, lick them, bite them hard because however hard I bit, they were lips that never fell apart. And the bloody gum trying to depart his white teeth, a gum I kept sucking all the time. But he didn't want me to stop at his lips. He told me to pull the shutters down and go to bed with him. His legs stuck out over the end they were so long, his was a body that exceeded mine from head to toe. He spoke a language I didn't understand while he moved as if he didn't know how, as if we were adolescents and didn't know how to guide the impulses spurred by desire from lack of experience. What *was* he saying? Lovely loving words and flattery or nasty insults? I could recall them now, but I'd never dare go and ask for a translation, even if I knew the name of the language he used. Can you imagine me trying? No, much better to keep that unknown litany to myself and imagine what it meant. He soon poked it in and I'd forgotten the little English I'd learned at secondary school, the language the Ghanaian had used with Mr Ethereal, so I was astonished when a cry came from deep inside me, an 'Oh, my God' that sounded absurd even before it became audible. I was too short to take him all in, every thrust made the pain unbearable, as if he was shredding my insides. We weren't made to measure even though I tried to find the pleasure he thought the experience should be giving me. The bigger, the better, the women said at work. Yes, you say, but life isn't a porn film, though in theory I was in the most arousing situation possible. I put up with the pain and with him moving on top of me as if it was the first time he'd touched a woman. The emotion caused by his explorations soon subsided and I was happy to have his sooty body on top of mine and smell an armpit from the tropics.

It was no sacrifice not to repeat the experience. Maybe if I'd given him a second opportunity, it might have been better, we'd have both learned to go at the same rhythm, to rock at the same pace, but he rushed and spoiled it. One day he turned up with a small box wrapped up in shiny paper that I found quite upsetting. So small in a hand that was so large... I don't know if I was sorrier on his behalf or mine, but I told him as best I could that he didn't need to buy me anything, that he shouldn't have got me a present, he really shouldn't, but he was all nervous, as if he'd felt duty bound. When I opened it, after I'd removed the wrinkled silken paper, I found a trinket on a chain that was as thin as fishing line. It was orange and square and darker at one corner. There were also earrings made from the same material. He said he wanted to marry me, we could go to the United States and live with his brother, where they'd given him a study scholarship and look after children who had no parents or parents who couldn't look after them. Not to say it might not have been a nice adventure, him being so tender, but I've never believed in tenderness that comes so easily, and even less so if we'd already fucked. You, sir, must know this well enough, what men like is guaranteed sex: sex they can have on tap whenever they need it, and a lot think that a trinket on a fishing line is enough to guarantee them a woman who is always up for anything. Though frankly nothing he might have offered would have been enough. Not at the time.

the Extremaduran

I think He encouraged me to go after the young guy from Extremadura so I would tell Him about it, but I wasn't altogether sure. Imagine, then, how long my adventure with Him has gone on for. Much longer than I sometimes like to remember. It's typical of this kind of relationship, they are so on and off that you don't notice the time passing and they become part of your life even though it's only one fuck after another. They are tricky because those that are only sex shouldn't be an affair at all, should be simply loose pieces of a mosaic that makes up your sexual CV. If it is longer than one of these fragments it's because we're not just talking sex. But if what went on with Him wasn't only sex, I couldn't tell you exactly what it was. The fact is that I got on the train to go back to my city after dark and sat on one of those fold-up seats by the doors that open and shut in every station. Have you ever noticed the squeaky noise they make when they fold down? It puts my teeth on edge. Luckily the train emptied out and I could move to one of the fixed seats. The conductor who was wearing a striped shirt and a name badge came by and asked to see my ticket. I was simply struck by his smile. Now I can only recall the chaos of bodies from when I went from one to another and couldn't say which was the last or whose smell was lingering on my skin. I kept telling myself that was complete freedom, that I was doing what I wanted to do, much more than other women who were so repressed. Can you imagine, sir, how I could split myself in two like that and do nothing to salvage myself from the anguish beginning to silt up my forearms? I'd sit there and smell my arm trying to guess who'd impregnated me most, but the residues got all mixed up and I couldn't even identify my own. All to show Him what I was capable of or conceal from Him things that were less congenial. Yes, you're right, I didn't really want to show Him how far I could go. In fact, I wasn't into revealing anything.

I was still sniffing my skin when the Extremaduran, who was the ticket inspector, sat opposite me and started talking as if I knew him. He got the shakes because he was sure I fancied him. I hadn't registered that until then, but he sat down to talk and immediately said I was very pretty. Saying which was like a first step in the protocol, a statement of intent, like compliments from building workers, though a lot politer. And entirely neutral, practically meaningless, in fact, doesn't mean lovely (a word more to do with love) or hot (more to do with sex). Pretty is a no-risk comment, unless you react with a different kind of gaze, that's that, because it's simply a compliment. Not hot, you're hot is bold and the person saying it has to be very confident or can end up looking quite ridiculous. As I gestured to catch the Extremaduran's attention, in what was a counter-attack, he soon shifted from pretty to you're so pretty, that showed he was teetering on the brink, or trying to keep up polite appearances.

The Extremaduran was on the short side, and his hair went from very patchy light ash to white. In fact, he wasn't *that* different, not one of those different guys I'd have chosen at the time. When he saw I didn't reject him out of hand he got even more nervy, just went to and fro from the door when the train stopped, and I struck a pose I'd have thought absurd if I could have seen myself from the outside. I remember taking a wisp of hair and twisting it round a finger, but I don't remember ever deciding to do that. Why did I do what every woman does when they are flirting? Had I always done that? I leaned my head to one side and smiled, looking deep into his eyes. No, not really, I'd only just met him, but I acted up as if I were coming on to him. Did I? When did I start? If only I'd known then how difficult it is to identify one's own needs. I don't know if it was him or the excitement I felt in a situation that seemed straight out of a film more than anything else. Travelling, moving around, had always stirred me up, and even more so that evening when I was walking the world and mingling my body smell with lots of others.

He went from the shakes and how pretty you are to suggesting we go to the lavatory at the back of the train, as he leaned his elbows on his knees, looking first at the ground and then looking up and suggesting that. So what do you think, he asked yours truly, who was sitting very comfortably thank you, because it's one thing to grease the path, and another not to respect the necessary pauses and gambits. Yes, I know it sounds laughable given the circumstances, but I can assure you that even the most sudden entanglement has its tempo. The fact was the smells of other men were so disgusting I told myself that would be one way of shedding them before I could get home and have a shower. At each stop he pressed the button by the side of the door and said 'end of operation'. That meant nobody was getting on or off and the train could move off again. After that I took note of other inspectors and I never saw them do that or use those words that seemed straight out of a spy film.

I walked through the coaches in between half-empty seats, taking care not to fall when there was a jolt and I sensed people were watching me. It was rather shocking to be walking behind the inspector on a day when there were so few passengers. We talked as we walked and people looked at us and must have thought it was strange, I bet, and I imagined they all guessed what was on the cards. You won't be surprised to hear how that little stroll turned me on, as you know how fond I was, sickeningly so, of a little exhibitionism. Perhaps not so sickeningly, but I ask you. Sometime after that I made the mistake of opening a lavatory door I'd mistaken for the door to the next carriage and had to shut it quickly when I saw a young girl sitting on top of an inspector with his trousers at half-mast. I totally understood and smiled as I recalled my trip with the man from Extremadura.

I don't actually remember the trip inside the lavatory, perhaps because of the residues from previous bodies on mine that I've already mentioned or because they were such hectic days I don't recall anything at all very clearly. It's scary to think there are corners of myself that are lost forever. Part of me that will never return, isn't that horrible? Now I just see images, and blink at their content as I had never done before, saturated as I was by the breath of other men and by so much saliva that wasn't mine that I just didn't want to know, I simply wanted to be done with that train as soon as possible so I could run and tell Him. But he decided to stick his tongue in my mouth at some point, a white one that tasted curious, that I'd anticipated when he was talking to me and spit had trickled from the corner of his lips. I don't know if I found it unpleasant, but I kept looking away so as not to taste it. He was in a rush to put his hand on my cunt and go straight to the pleasure trigger, I suppose he wanted to finish it off quickly but I've never liked people imposing orgasms on me, and organizing them as if they were practising after an anatomy class. It reminded me of school: the clitoris is here and if you rub it awhile you'll come. Instructions as if it was an electrical appliance. Anyone would think that men went from doing it through a hole in a sheet to doing it with an anatomy chart they'd got from a cheap magazine. Or from school, with those horrid drawings of pink vulva slits. Please do inform all the gentlemen you know: we women aren't appliances with a button between the legs you can press to switch us on. Well, you know all that and so do I now, but then I just thought he was clueless. There were times when I started to wonder whether men existed who weren't rough like that, began to wonder if I wasn't to blame for falling in with the clueless of this world who just stuck a finger in, not even bothering to remove your wet skin with their nails. At any rate I did come in the lavatory in the last carriage en route to my city, either because it was the right day in the month, or so I could forget all those previous bodies or maybe it was the sight of the landscape receding into the night. That was a poetic vision, perhaps the only detail that made that encounter unforgettable, that meant it wasn't totally pathetic. That memory will stay with me forever, the speed at which I rushed away from the darkness dotted with stars that seemed to be rushing me away from myself. A memorable scene that I should have experienced with someone who was at least slightly more than a name emblazoned on a badge. Yes, you are right, sir, life isn't a porn film. Sometimes, in spite of everything, I think it's much better than that.

Perhaps it's why I suffered a sudden attack of selfishness, as if I was in retreat from men. It wasn't so much then, but I started not to be worried about *their* pleasure. I needed to punish them but didn't know what crime they'd committed. Perhaps if I'd known what my own complaint was, that I didn't want what they did or didn't do to me, I could have told them. When I woke up from the union with everything that orgasm brings… don't laugh, it's true, orgasm is about being united with the world and completely forgetting oneself. So when I woke up from one, I felt lonelier than ever but the pain was even worse and that made me want to erase the last few minutes, rewind to when he asked me if I wanted to go to the lavatory and I'd said no, thanks all the same. In some film or TV series they called it the seventh-floor effect. When all you want to do is throw yourself off a seventh floor. And what can I say? I didn't know then that what I wanted to say was no and that's why I left them halfway. How was I to know that, if I was the one doing what she felt like? Perhaps that was what my reproach was about, that in fact I wanted to say no when I let them lead me on, but at the time it wouldn't have made much sense to complain. They weren't to blame either, or at least, only partly. The guy from Extremadura, the poor dupe, said now me, now me. No, I replied, I don't feel like it and he got desperate with his hard-on, you can't leave me like this, *mujer*, he wailed in Spanish, *no puedes dejarme así*. I just had the sense to retort, laughing to hide my own grief: end of operation.

But don't get me wrong, that incident left me with a very pleasant aftertaste. Not what you would call sweet, because I still feel upset when I think of his body, but I sometimes see the Extremaduran when I take the train, sometimes I'm by myself and sometimes with other people. I see him and he is always laughing and he says if you ever want anything, just let me know. That journey ended in my city and he invited me to his hotel but I'd worked in the hotel and knew that they always gave the train drivers and inspectors the small bedroom right at the end of the corridor, with a single bed under a sloping ceiling lower than any other, as if it was an attic.

the Punjabi

I also met the Punjabi on the train. I know, you must think it odd so many things happen to me on trains, but what more can I say? It's a space containing lots of people, that moves at top speed, and speed, as you must know, makes it easier to take decisions you're not sure you want to take. Like when you're drinking or dancing. When the train moves off, it's almost as if I forget what I'm hoping to be, cast off all my phobias and let myself go. I think I was struck by the Punjabi's broad-boned forehead and deep-set, sombre eyes framed by black lashes. He always travelled with another colleague whose face I don't recall and used the train when I worked in that supermarket twenty minutes from my city. I didn't like supermarket work one bit, I preferred cleaning and I only lasted three weeks. I went there in a month when it was already very hot and I had to cut meat in a freezing room with one of those glass walls through which you could see the customers walking by. It was as good as a frozen goldfish bowl. I don't know if I could still do what I learned to do so easily there: take a whole sheep and cut it up into chunks placed in order on trays, ready for Sunday barbecues. You know how strident noise really upsets me, and when I remember how I used to grab the sheep by two legs,

I can't imagine how I stood the noise the blade made when it sliced through the dead animal's bones. Not to mention the real horrors my unscrupulous manager did with the meat. Everyone knows about this kind of thing, right? Well, it was quite routine, really: the moment we arrived in the morning, our first task was to salvage from the freezer all the packets whose sell-by-date was that day, strip the plastic off and wrap them up again as if they were fresh that day, putting the sell-by date back another week. Naturally I've already told you how I have tried other jobs that aren't cleaning, and how they didn't work out. In the end I have no choice but to clean, because I like cleaning up other people's worlds. Don't you laugh! Everything has its place in this life. What I most disliked about that job were the smells, the mixture of the industrial disinfectant we sloshed over the floor, the damp cardboard boxes stacked at the back of the store, and the meat daubed with barbecue sauce to hide the stench of rotten flesh. When I clambered on the train straight from the cold store, the sun blistered my face and I felt like all my blood was about to pour out. As it was a factory town, we always saw the same people at the same time. The Punjabi had caught my eye some time ago and I was aroused by the polite, if cheeky, way he stared me in the eye and declared his intent. This also changes from country to country, you know? Depending on where they come from, men are more or less daring when they look at you. At the time I deflected his interest in me by showing an interest in the landscape, that was lovely, no doubt about that, but maybe not so lovely as to make me keep returning to it when I needed relief from the intensity in the Punjabi's eyes. That guy knew how to look at you, and some! So I started to imagine him as a child learning from adults in his country how to make a woman steam with desire simply with a look whenever the carriage jolted, such intensity, eye control to drive a woman crazy. As if we were eye-fucking, as if the gaze was all the contact necessary, the whole bit. Do you think I'm exaggerating? If only you could have heard my heart beat on that journey, my veins, my capillaries pounding with a deafening noise. I imagined my Punjabi inside a packed train learning how to look at women the way he looked at me that day, with other Indians hanging off the ladders or the roof and a scent of spices wafting over the fields. But don't think that all men are skilled in such a subtle art, the men in my city never have been. The Punjabi's eyes showed he liked me, I could read in them all the things he would like to do with me if he had me in bed, if he could touch me. I knew the ritual from the day he sat opposite me: look away, look back, act as if your eyes meet by chance. Until one day, quite unaware of what we were like and never having exchanged a word, we spent the whole journey staring into each other's eyes. We said nothing, simply gazed at each other non-stop, not acknowledging we were gazing at each other, and his colleague next to him who didn't know where to put himself. He spoke to him and got an answer now and then but never a look, because he was fully occupied looking at me. I'd never have said that sex could be aired that way. That was sex for real although it was all in the eyes. The smell of him went up my nose and straight to the bottom of my belly, not to my crotch, just above it, the area of the belly that touches the bone in the middle of the pelvis. It was a nice present, don't you think? A smell to make you tingle right there. I became conscious of my breathing as I gazed at him. The way he parted his lips from time to time so I could see a wet tongue that was saying I'm waiting for you. The whole of him cried out I'm waiting for you, waiting for you to come to me. My whole body was aimed at him, like iron particles drawn to a magnet, rushing pell-mell to satisfy it, my nipples aimed his way, my neck kept telling me to lean backwards and forget the world, forget everything, yet again. That was on a day when the train was full, people were sitting and standing everywhere, but I'd forgotten where I was some time ago, was deep in his eyes that were transporting me elsewhere. I crossed my legs that were threatening to explode there and then and splatter everyone, but I never fled his gaze. He looked as if he wanted to say something because the train was approaching its destination when I returned to the landscape, closed my eyes and let out one last sigh, and I felt the final shudders from my orgasm like a snake wriggling in and out of me.

He looked at me, taken aback. We no longer shared the same state of arousal, I was now somewhere else and for a moment was sorry I'd moved far from him, as if we were suddenly both alone, distanced from each other, though I was the one who'd created that distance. The train was coming to a halt and the colour of his eyes had been out of control for some time, his eyes darted here and there, and he was rubbing his leg, hitting his heels on the floor, forcing a grimace that wanted to break into a smile. Until finally he said despairingly, 'Will you come?' I immediately said yes, which is what I said whenever I could, you know, you have to live your life, make the most of it in case one day, when I'm walking peacefully along the street, a car crashes into me, and I'll regret not doing everything I wanted to do. It took me so long to realise that what I was doing in fact was gradually killing myself off, so convinced was I that fucking the first comer I fancied was the way to get the most joy out of life.

We walked down the familiar backstreets of my city, with people I knew looking at me and him holding my hand, rushing, turning round now and then to smile happily. When I think about that now, he seems to have a child's face. When I remember him like that, I feel quite warm and tender, as if, despite the circumstances, there'd been some contact with him beyond the search for pure pleasure, beyond our bodies. Once you've said yes to men they always look as if they can't believe what's happening and at the same time you can see a terrible fear deep in their eyes, that's well hidden by their euphoria. Yes, I know you always laugh when I say that I scare men, but you won't deny there isn't some truth in what I'm saying. Maybe it was that kind of mystery I was after. Or he was after because I didn't know if they could see my own fear.

The Punjabi melded into me down those narrow streets until we reached an old house, three flights of stairs that seemed to move, steps deformed by so many years of use, strange smells from strange kitchens and orange butane gas bottles lined up under rusty blue metal post boxes that may have been almost green. Scraps of paper, supermarket special offers next to the bottles and a young kid's damaged pushchair under the stairs. I remember having to duck my head in order to go up, but perhaps that's only what I'm remembering now, you know how memory is as deceptive as we want it to be. I hardly ever went to men's houses, I preferred them to come to mine, so I felt safe though I was never afraid they might hurt me. I would look at it from the outside and think it might have been safer to be afraid, you can't always be giving yourself up to strangers, they might be psychopaths who tie you up and rape you once you were in their house. But excitement always got the better of any fear I might have had. So in that spirit I entered his house and his kitchen-diner with a green, flowery oilskin on the table, and strewn with empty cartons and plastic bags. That's all I remember, the plastic bags everywhere, by the cooker, filling the empty space between the fridge and the wall, inside another bag hanging from a hook near the greasy window. Men living alone, sure, but why all that plastic? He cleared a space on the table, cleaned it with a washed-out cloth and asked me if I was hungry. When he spoke his tongue curled back and clicked against his top teeth. I hadn't expected that, I didn't understand why he was distracting me with nonsense like offers of food. Why weren't we in his bed right now or on top of that table there? Could it be that after the excitement of the gaze, I wasn't that exciting anymore? He did seem aroused as he sliced up some fruit and put it on a plate, but I needed him to get on with it fast, as if he couldn't curb his desire to get inside me another second. When men took their time over that, over stripping me without so much as a by your leave, I'd start to ask myself uncomfortable questions that would put a brake on *my* desire. Rather than crushing me, the Punjabi said 'like that' as he put salt on the fruit. I found salt on fruit off-putting. I liked to eat things I'd not tasted before, but salted fruit was too way out. He put several pakoras on a glass dish: these are hot! And his tongue started clicking quickly, when he made tea. I'd lost the desire and didn't know what to do. Ask him what his name was? Where he came from? How old he was? I was feeling increasingly ill at ease in that house that was drowning me in plastic when all I wanted was a fuck. Until he started eating and took a bottle of ketchup from the fridge. *Esto bueno con pakora*, he went on in Spanish. And his 'r' sounded very different but I was quite disenchanted, the disenchantment that comes from the sight of such an exotic dish smothered with something as ordinary as ketchup.

the Galician

I've met lots of Galicians working in that factory, but I found mine in a club a long way from the city where I live, and that's why I did such different things with him. Well, you know, sir, maybe not *that* different, please don't start imagining anything outlandish. I told him I'd a way of spotting Galicians, whether he wanted to believe me or not; by that time I'd developed a special knack that allowed me to detect them. *You* don't believe me? I tell you I can, if I'm in a crowd, I can pick them out a mile off. Sure, I know they're not so different, but they've got traits in common. Lots are swarthy, black-haired, round-faced, but you also get fair-haired, thin-faced, bright-eyed specimens. You can't find words for what makes them alike, because it's nothing specific, it's a particular manner they have. OK, maybe I've imagined this Galician bit, but not entirely, I tell you.

    I bumped into my Galician at the bar when I turned round and my arm brushed against his. He smiled and asked me in Spanish: what do you bet we were born the same day? I couldn't hear him and let myself be carried away by the music. The beers I'd drunk were making me light or heavy-headed, as if I couldn't feel my weight or whether my body was mine or belonged to someone else. You forget your body after a couple of drinks, and can do whatever you want with it, as if it was no longer your own. Which is the whole point of getting drunk, right? I felt he was so close I could smell his breath, and his hair was falling over his eyes as if he were half asleep. So what do I get if it turns out we were born on the same day? That's not possible, I replied. The eighteenth of March, *el dieciocho de marzo*, I said as slowly as I could, emphasising the 'th' and the 'ch'. The kind of thing that makes men go wild, wherever they come from. There you are, me too! I called him a liar, said what a roundabout way to pick up a girl, trying to be original and that I didn't believe him for one minute. He took out his ID card and showed it to me. Hey, it's not the same month, day or year! Sorry, I sometimes forget when my birthday is. I was still looking at his ID card when he started to sniff the roots of my hair behind one ear while his hair tickled my shoulder and cheek. His long black hair fell down like a curtain. I tried to smell the fatty smell the roots of his hair gave off, you know, the fatty, almost imperceptible smell greasy hair gives off at the end of the day, that makes it stick to your face if you don't wash it the next morning.

He pressed his nose into the folds of flesh behind my ear, doing it on purpose, as if trying to insert it and I resisted. Didn't you know some men want to get inside you even where there's no hole around? He slurped and sniffed, sucked my smell up and let out a long, affected sigh. He started to mutter indecent stuff, the things he would do to me, but he wasn't exactly stylish, because you *can* say such things with style. Or perhaps it was too soon to get so personal, using coarse remarks more likely to shake me out of the haze I was in and that's why I put a finger on his lips when he said your cunt's all wet or I'm going to fuck you here and now. He wasn't turning me on, was being too in your face, reminding me too much of the real situation. I'd been there before, knew what he was after, but I made an effort to make the scene more attractive, to give his clumsy misfiring a poetic touch and find something out of the ordinary to define the moment. You'll think it strange, but by now you must have seen how good I am at retrieving moments other people would rather forget. But obviously, if the guy is set on filling the chit-chat between two players with crude expressions like 'I'll stick it right the way up you', nobody can stop the fantasy slipping away as if by magic. And no way do I mean soft porn fantasy, I mean, it's about having a little respect for the other person involved. If I'd have known that, then...

I recall some men by their flesh, by their size, by the way they fill my space and seem to draw me towards their own bodies. Some had so much hair I stopped worrying about my own. I loved trying to meet their needs, loved them being so immediate and real, I loved to feel them weighing me down, squashing me and making me feel small to the point that I disappeared. Gripping my love handles and never letting go, feeling safe, tight up against them, as if I could never drown. *He* was like that, all body. Pity I never got to that stage with my Galician, I never felt his weight on me. I had to make do with hugging his huge belly in one of those lavatory stalls where we cracked the bowl. How did *that* happen? What did we do to make us feel a sudden splash of water under our feet and us laughing our heads off? I still don't know whether it was spurting from some pipe or other we'd not seen or whether it was awash before we got there. We didn't do anything different, he went on kneeling in the water which might have been dirty, for all we knew, gripping my legs, leaving red circles that faded when his chubby fingers stopped squeezing me and he surfaced for a breath of air. My palms slipped on the lavatory walls as I tried to stop keeling over. The water was refreshing.

We left the lavatory and looked for that friend of his. All I remember about him is that he was bald and dark-skinned, though not enough to make me think he was from abroad, and that his eyes bulged right out of their sockets, and I was in between them drinking and the Galician talking to his friend, who obviously knew we'd gone to the lavatory to do what we'd done. The Galician, his trousers sopping wet, stuck his tongue deep inside my mouth, inside my ear, as he looked at his friend and I followed his gaze to his friend who told us he'd tried to get off with a waitress and that she'd turned him down. You know what, he acted as if he'd been insulted, – I was the one who didn't want her; her breath stank. She's tasty, but when I got near her and she opened her mouth I stepped back, felt sick. For my part I felt reassured by these two bodies close to me, as if I was inside a container that could hold me at the same time as a big crowd. When the Galician took his tongue out of my ear, he left a cold sensation that lasted until his saliva dried up.

The Galician hugged me from behind in front of his friend, and when he did that, I thought why not. Why not? What the hell, I'm me and it's my body. Why not? You and I talked a lot about that question of mine, afterwards, didn't we, sir? And it took a long time to come up with an answer. He kissed me, bit my lips and sucked them away from my gums, ran his tongue around my neck and pinched my bum hard. I only realized that he was doing it hard the next morning, when I saw the purple circles in the mirror. He was feeling my breasts all over in front of his friend, who was all eyes in that heaving club. After which he pulled me over to his friend, and now the three of us were touching, their legs wrapped round mine and both breathing hard on me, the Galician with his warm tongue and teeth all over my neck and his hands on my breasts till he'd pulled the material away, till I was completely naked in front of his gawping friend. Maybe they'd done a deal, but the other guy had only eyes for what the Galician was offering him. And I was what was on offer. I expect you're shocked, right, sir? That's why I'm telling you because you're the only person I could tell. I tell you there's nothing so nice as the lightness you feel when you know your will is in someone else's hands, you can't imagine how carefree you are when you are relieved of life's ugly burden. He was the one doing what he wanted with me and I wasn't the one taking decisions. He grabbed me by the back of the neck and yanked my breast out, looking deep into his friend's eyes, as if saying look what I've got for you but I knew he'd never touch me however close he got. He was swigging beer when he saw the Galician almost pushing me on to him, the cold bottle against my skin, the froth running down my neck to one of my nipples and in between my breasts. The beer forked down two paths.

Later on we left and went to another club crammed with even more bodies, but it's all a very hazy memory. I only know we went to his place, that just the two of us went up in the lift, that he had other friends in the other club and I could smell their smells all around me, I don't know if they touched me, if they hugged me, if I got too close to them. And you won't believe this, however much I'd like to put all that behind me, I'm still upset by the fact I don't really remember what they did to me.

At his place I felt something give inside me, I thought it must be all that excitement. He'd left me in bed, a very clean, wooden bed with normal, everyday sheets. Almost all men, whatever strange things they like doing, use standard sheets that make you think about their daily routines, how they strip them off and put them to wash, how they fold and flatten them, how they make their bed before going out, or don't when they're in a hurry. All men, wherever, keep some kind of secret you really don't want to find out. My Galician had left me there and I took the opportunity to run my finger through the liquid that had oozed into my knickers to see what it was like. I turned up a sticky swab of red blood I rolled between my fingers for a while. I know that you, sir, won't find this disgusting: after all it was only blood from my body. I like to look at my blood, like when you cut yourself and wait for it to bubble up on your skin. I told him we'd have to stop, tittering and gesticulating with my fingers, I told him I was out of action. You mean you've got your period, he asked in Spanish. So what, I registered that when I sucked up some of your blood, very tasty it was too, *riquísima*. My head buzzed and felt revolted, but I was too drunk to think much about him. Our rhythm dropped off, our movements slowing down when he was inside me, when we were side by side because neither of us could go on top. It was really nice doing it in slow motion, with him talking slowly and both of us moaning away.

I didn't give the Galician my telephone number. I reckoned he was peculiar, his way of showing affection *was* peculiar. I fell asleep while he was still inside me and when he slipped out my blood ran all down my thighs to my knees, bright red, first-day blood. I remember him putting my head on the pillow, fetching a wet towel I could feel on the soft skin on the inside of my thighs, I remember him running his fingers through my hair, as if he were combing it, his hand flat on my cheek, and him kissing me on the arm, a kiss that wasn't the kiss of a one-night stand.

the Englishman

The Englishman and I were ever so slightly in love, if you can know what being in love means or the circumstances required to say you are in love. Place was important in this whole affair, where we met and where we'd get to know each other even better later on: the factory's fermentation room. I used to clean out the dry dough balls that had dropped off the long chain of rimmed platters where they put them before they came out of that stifling heat and were flattened into pizza shape. The heat meant nobody liked going near the fermenting, but I preferred it to being by the oven with the stone bases that kept circling around. Whenever I'd thought of that brand of pizza I'd imagined the country farmhouse on the wrapper, not the grandpa and the children in the advert, but the farmhouse itself. And the oven was definitely made of stone, but it was an enormous machine where pizzas went in and then came out a few minutes later, close to each other, on square pieces of stone. The entrance to the oven was what I really loathed, where the dough piled up and was as dry as anything, all mixed up with tomato, and covering the light green cables we had to pull out by hand, that we couldn't get really clean even with the hoses. I liked the fermenting room because it was so warm and because we only had to remove the dough balls and sweep up, there was never ever any water inside there. Plenty of flour though, that fell on your face when you got under the production line with all those balls patiently waiting to inflate.

You always sweat in the fermenting rooms. That's why you always go in wearing only a blue overall with nothing underneath and green wellington boots that made your toes go plop-plop. The day I met the Englishman, I didn't know he was inside. There was a silence that absorbed all the other noises in the factory though, from a distance, as if the dough was really isolated from the rest of the world, as if they'd padded the walls so the dough didn't take fright. A line manager told me that without that silence the pizza bases would go hard, dry and lifeless, that the noise outside *would* frighten them. That wasn't true, there was silence because it was one of the few places in the factory that was sealed, like an endlessly long room. I walked to the back to start clearing out the dough that had stuck to my soft boots that I usually wore without socks because I'd be in a rush and leave them in a tangle on the sofa. That was why it wasn't at all odd I didn't see the Englishman until I was right at the back, lying on the ground wearing steel toe-caps, blue trousers and a shirt. That was the difference between a mechanic and a cleaning lady: we wore an overall and they wore two items of clothing, though all in the same colour. I don't know if the Englishman was a mechanic or engineer or something of the sort: I could only see his legs.

Nobody knows what makes that fermenting smell, as if it's something alive, that's rancid and living at the same time, if you get too much it smells like something rotten. And that day it came mixed up with the black grease from the machine's cogs and the smell of the guy underneath whose face I'd still not seen. Anyone who gets in there with someone else was bound to feel turned on, anyone would. I kneeled down next to the guy, who still hadn't seen me. Till I got tired of skulking and cleared my throat. My memories are a blur from then on. How did we make first contact? Did we say hello? Did we shake hands? Did he come out from underneath and bang his head he was so surprised like in a gag in some awful farce? Did we look deep into each other's eyes as if it were love at first sight? I don't remember, but you can bet it wasn't the latter. I only retain flashes of what happened: the taut sinews supporting the weight of his body when he still didn't know I was there, stretched out on my front under the machines, struggling to prise off dry dough that gave off that stench of fermenting, of rotting when it came away, and him walking over me in that narrow corridor to fetch his tools, stooping because he was so tall, and me splattered with flour that he tried to wipe off my cheek, without saying a word. I do remember that, his caress and his excuses. Sir, if only you knew the times I've been caressed by men who weren't even aware of what they were doing, weren't staking any claims. Caresses escape your control, though you try to put the brake on, your hands are insistent, need to do it.

Then there was supper on Friday with all the other workers, though not the personnel that made the pizzas, only the casual labour, the mechanics and cleaners. Fridays spent racing with trolleys full of cheese and ham, sharing pizzas we couldn't eat during the rest of the week. What sweet revenge on the managers who threw them away when they'd just been packaged if they fell on the ground but wouldn't let us eat them. Or did let us, if we asked their permission, like dogs waiting outside the door to be thrown scraps. Such subtle, invisible humiliation. It was also one of those Fridays when we went to a bar that opened early and drank and drank, he more than me and he was so huge he wrapped all around me. And then we walked to my place and, in the middle of a square, stared deep into each other's eyes in a scene that could be straight out of a film. His eyes were bloodshot and watery, and he pretended to be very emotional, or really was, who knows? We were on the point of kissing when he stopped me, his mouth close to mine, turned my chin towards the sky so we could see the moon and said in Spanish *¡Mira todo!* Look at all that! You only have a first kiss once and I want you to remember every detail forever. Our first kiss was a heavy, sultry effort, our legs went this way and that as the sun began to make us realize how pathetic we must seem. We went into my bedroom, closed the shutters to keep out the light of day and let the weight of our bodies crash down.

Sex with the Englishman was also perfect, pity it was a swindle, an illusion, because it wasn't ever really him and he acted as if it was a great love affair. Obviously, you've guessed that I didn't see it like that at the time. I could only laugh at his bouts of drunken romanticism. I love you, he kept repeating in English, I'll always love you, and he went on talking though I didn't understand a word. Perhaps we did love each other a bit by virtue of repeating the word so often. Or perhaps not, because by this time it's quite obvious that however much you repeat clichéd words it doesn't make an event as improbable as love actually happen. That first night that had turned into day I was surprised the Englishman kept at it so long. He was at least twenty years older than me and was very drunk, but it didn't seem to affect him. He knew all about rhythm, and that made him a better lover than others, he knew about ritual and took it step by step, but I just felt like a good sleep after a whole evening at work and an early morning round of drinking. The bed didn't have a head board at the time and I missed not being able to hold on to one. They say beds without one aren't a good idea, probably because you have nothing to hold on to when you need to. I gripped the bedroom wall knowing I'd leave finger marks while I felt my head spinning and wanted to tell him to stop once and for all, that I'd had enough. But the Englishman, like so many others, also wanted to impose pleasure on me. You, sir, must know that lots of men are like that. And it's as if they do what they've always done with women but in reverse: instead of not worrying about us coming they now force us to have orgasms, in part to satisfy themselves, I suppose. That night I felt his snores and body next to me, an almost transparent white body where you could see the blood in the veins under his skin.

The Englishman only visited occasionally from another factory, in a country the name of which I don't remember, and lived in a hotel when he was staying in my city and luckily it wasn't the hotel where I had worked that had a small bedroom for train ticket inspectors. It was a different one with rooms with a small kitchen where the Englishman cooked Thai food for me on a Saturday when I slept over. It was sad living in a hotel, with the clothes he'd washed in the bath hanging on a small clothes hanger on one side of the bedroom, with that sort of curtain at the foot of the bed to separate the living room from where he slept. I had more than one nightmare there. I remember his big, white tongue that he stuck everywhere, his eyes that every so often looked like a child's, his arms that were very long like the Ghanaian's, his fingers as well and the unusual way his back curved. Did you know that backs curve differently depending on which country you come from?

The Englishman started to distance himself gradually, without making a fuss. It was like a normal relationship, going for a drink together, sleeping together on Saturdays, dancing and all that, having breakfast together on Sunday, and me so used to doing that by myself. However, he had a melodramatic side that I discovered was triggered by alcohol. You are afraid to say I love you, he'd keep saying, upset because I'd never actually told him I did. No, I wasn't afraid, I just didn't love him. Perhaps he thought I did from the way I gave myself up to him, from the caresses I let escape, that my hands were to blame for, from the way I gazed at him when he was falling asleep, but they are things I've done with every man I've ever been with. You will probably think it rather trite if I tell you how the need to love slips from my fingers however much I try to put the brake on, you'll probably think it absurd if I tell you I put the brake on because, deep down, I didn't believe in that whole affair. I'm not sure, that's how I see it now, but at the time I just didn't feel like saying I love you, and wanted to laugh when he did.

I found a bottle of small blue pills in his bathroom and saw he was desperate, suddenly impotent, the day he had none left. It's harder to get them here, because he didn't have a local doctor. Maybe these blue pills have sorted lots of problems for you older men, but I can tell you now that I felt let down. However, it was no big deal, sometimes you don't even have to finish an affair: they sometimes end all by themselves. He went back to that country in Europe that wasn't his or mine and we never exchanged another word, not even on New Year's Day when you send a message to everyone on your list of contacts.

the Blind Man

If I told you I went with a blind man you'd maybe imagine a tremendous love story built on real feelings that go beyond appearances, defeating all kinds of hurdles, but ours was simply a miserable night out that wasn't even sad, and depressingly didn't even teeter on the tragic. In fact, it was far from romantic. Not that I was looking for any sort of romance, it's just that when I say I once went with a blind man, from the outset it seems as if I'm setting up a story that will minimally touch the heart strings. However, don't get it wrong, I didn't go to bed with him because I felt sorry or because he intuited something in me that other men didn't, I did it because he was the same as the others and partly from guilt and partly, I have to admit, out of curiosity.

Street parties are more drunken than the indoor variety. I met my Blind Man at a summer party. I was at a packed party in a square with blaring music when I noticed him standing next to me with his stick, angrily asking them to serve him a Coke. He turned to me and said that they'd brought their own rum and I kept shouting, come on, come on, you are so slow, we've been waiting for ages. We were being pushed and shoved and it was a struggle not to be swept aside by the crowd, to keep one elbow on the counter where they were serving drinks. How are you, lovely? Having a good time? Sure, are you? Well, I'm dying of thirst and these bastards won't serve me. I still don't know how the conversation continued or why I came out with 'so what's the stick for, you off to climb a mountain?' Believe me, I'd never have said that if I hadn't been drunk. In fact, I still go bright red when I remember. No, I'm blind, he replied. I thought he was joking and I burst out laughing, the kind of laugh that dries up, congeals and freezes in some part of your head, then shrinks and pricks like a splinter however much you try to act as if nothing's wrong and keep up what is now hollow laughter. All I could think to say was that he didn't seem blind. After that, I stuck close to him for the whole night.

I kept gulping beer down to douse my wretched feeling of guilt, while the Blind Man and I spoke about this and that, as if nothing was amiss, as if I hadn't put my foot in it, as if he wasn't blind. He cracked unfunny jokes about blind men and said I was a real turn on. And how do you know? I asked, intrigued to see if I could catch a touch of the mystic in him. I just know you are, I know you are a real turn on, and I imagined he must get it through the nose as I do with men, particles get up your nostrils and drive you mad, scents from bodies that pursue you before they've got a clue. We sat down on a platform where his friend was clowning around, jumping up and down, while the Blind Man and I chatted. All barriers were down because the way things had gone so far I knew I'd dropped my guard and was simply curious to know what a man was like who couldn't see from close up – and that drove me towards him, the same curiosity I'd had for mechanics, ticket inspectors, ethereal types, Ghanaians or Punjabis. My curiosity for anyone I might think different, and the more the merrier. You, sir, may think I'm being frivolous, but I was in part attracted to men who were different because I was incredibly interested in finding out about them. As we talked, he kept running his hand over my shoulders, over my cheeks, but it wasn't the tender gesture I might have predicted, wasn't the gesture you see in films driven by a desire to know the other, a respectful move, wanting to know what you are like because he can't find out from looking at you. It wasn't remotely that kind of enquiring touch because I soon read other intentions in the chubby fingers of my Blind Man, who wasn't particularly supple in his movements and didn't know what to with his hands, who wanted to get acquainted with other areas of my skin and flesh and I was really keen to explore the skin of someone who explored me so avidly and wanted to get to know me by touching my skin but not tearing it at all. After the Englishman's onslaughts that weren't in the least metaphorical and hurt, now not even sex could save me from pain that was more intense than anything physical. I didn't look at myself once in the mirror the night I spent with the Blind Man, not even in the morning, and didn't even switch the lights on when I went to the lavatory.

When there was nobody else in the street and the town hall lorry was washing down the ground that was strewn with plastic glasses and bottles, with vomit and dirt from the frenzied stamping during the concert, the Blind Man asked me if I lived very far away. Not really, I replied, not really, though it's a bit uphill. We should talk to him, he said nodding towards where his friend was humming the last tune from the concert. He came over and stared at me trying to read my motives, as if I might hurt the Blind Man in some way. You sure everything is OK? he asked, putting a hand on his shoulder, and he replied right away that everything was fine. I insisted as well, saying I would see to everything, that he should come for him in the morning. I'll leave you my number just in case, I'll leave it switched on all night and tomorrow when you've had breakfast send me a text. Off you go, kid, and have a good time. It was as if I was taking him by force, as if literally he was a kid I was obliging to come with me and sleep away from home for the first time. We walked along and he gripped my arm and I followed the advice of his friend who'd said I should warn him when a step was coming up. A step, I'd say, and he'd go, I know, I know, because he wasn't completely blind.

But he certainly was completely blind in the pitch black in my house. While I pointed him along the corridor, while I didn't show him the rest of the flat, while we didn't need to switch the lights on. I was already used to walking in the dark, and had always done so to avoid the glare of naked bulbs. And that day, trying to be on equal terms, I didn't switch any lights on on the way to my bedroom, I wanted to see everything as he did. I thought that would be a nice thing to do.

The sex wasn't nice this time – yet again. Not in the slightest. He was as clumsy as other strangers. Strangers usually are, they usually go straight to the point maybe because they think that's what you want, maybe because you went straight to the point of getting off with them and they think you want that wild kind of sex when you hurl plates around the kitchen and strew paper over your office floor in order to clear your desk. They never imagine that if you take your time to say yes it may also be because you want good sex at the right rhythm, pauses, flow, alternating heavy clinches with gentle caresses, violent bites with fingering that is gentle and traces the contours of your body. No man seems to know this, but good sex is all about contrast. However, I now see it must be hard for them to understand that, because not even I understood what he wanted. I can tell you this now, but I don't know if he would have accepted a quiet romp. In fact, when anyone tried to elaborate the scenario for an encounter, I'd get stressed and go for the quick bang that would release me from the stress. I didn't want gaps between initial contact and sex, but then I wanted sex to be as good as the sex lifelong lovers enjoy. Yes, I know, I was being very contradictory but you know there were times when I was horribly mixed up.

And my Blind Man, no two ways about it, was a long way from being a good companion in bed. He wasn't intuitive, didn't feel my pulse, didn't have a better nose than men who can see what they were doing. He touched me frantically, went after my cavities as quickly as he could, his kisses were haphazard and what he said suddenly turned dirty. To begin with he did say, you are very beautiful, really beautiful. Words of love, I thought, as if I was part of the lyrics of some old-time song he was crooning, must be the sensitivity that blindness brings. How do you know if you can't see me? I asked while I laughed, still clinging to lyrical illusions. But he soon began to speak dirty, I bet you like to fuck, like it filthy, like it perverted and he mixed all that up with blind man jokes that weren't funny, it hurt and there was no way I could escape his nasty crude language, insults he reckoned would give me the hots. Hey, you're *una puta*, you like being called *una puta*, don't you? He was simply talking to himself and wanted no replies, I was merely a body to give him relief, but not like dominators. I'd make a sort of pact to surrender to them, they dominated me because I'd asked them to, and for that very reason there was respect. No, the insulting wasn't playful with my Blind Man, they were like attacks on women as such. I'd long since ceased to be beautiful. I should have thrown him out of my bed, should have pushed and shoved him out of my house, but I kept remembering his stick and my asking him if he was off up a mountain. I remembered how he couldn't go home at night if he didn't ring his friend and I didn't want to have to spend time with him in a temper waiting to be collected.

I should have guessed it would be like that from the moment he took his shoes off. The stink from his feet filling my bedroom was unbearable, made it impossible for me to smell him or get turned on. And shouldn't a man who's blind be more sensitive when it comes to listening and smelling? Couldn't he understand the stench of his feet was a horrible invasion of my senses?

The following morning his friend asked him how it had gone and he said fucking great, a fantastic lay, insisting I should ring him to set up another date. He even rang me a couple of times but then he must have realized I didn't want to repeat the experience.

the Moroccan

The Moroccan was blue. Yes, I know it's laughable how I remember people by their colour, but he was just what I said he is. No, he hadn't painted himself blue and wasn't like those men from the desert, it's just that when I try to remember him he always appears that colour. Maybe because of the way I met him, walking down the street in the middle of a big crowd when the sky was bright blue and dotted with clouds that seemed made from glistening white sugar. The Moroccan appeared in the jostling crowd, his bright eyes exactly the same colour as the sky. I looked at him and smiled, simply because I'd liked his eyes, that caught my attention among the dark overcoats he kept walking into. I smiled at him frankly, as if I'd never had a man before, suddenly certain I could smile at him and that would be that, I could gaze into those eyes that I liked and that would be an end to it. But it wasn't, obviously. After walking along still relishing an aftertaste of his blue, I heard a voice say, Wait. Wait, wait, don't be in such a hurry. As he hadn't sounded like a foreigner I was surprised he'd followed me: lots of men follow you down the street, but not men from here and with hair like mine, with eyes that didn't seem at all strange and dark brown hair, I didn't expect him to act differently. I felt taken aback that

I hadn't recognized a man who was my speciality because I'd not in fact spotted somebody different in the crowd.

I kept walking as I always do, as if people were chasing me and I was in flight, which I was in a way.

Then I recall a conversation in a café. How come I ended up there? He walked after me, asking me what my name was and I said it was none of his business with that laugh that slipped from the corner of my lips. I felt flattered he had pursued me for so long and immediately said yes when he asked me if I fancied a coffee. I remember him smiling a lot, but that was down to the sky that seemed straight out of a painting.

Then I remember turning the spoon round inside a cup with traces of white coffee he'd drunk, him talking a lot and talking really well, different *and* a good talker! He told me about his life, his family, and his travels. He had a handsome profile, but then I started thinking his forehead bulged far too much. My smile started to fade at the sight of that forehead. I no longer saw blue eyes, only forehead everywhere. Who's ever born like that? How can someone be born like that and how come I'd never noticed it before? In the meantime he talked and talked. He touched the back of my hand, gripped it tight and gazed at me silently. I could only laugh hysterically as in so many films when two people in love have held off declaring their love for so long, then suddenly can't not be together. Saccharine music cradles their gazes and gleaming light prevents them from hiding their emotions any longer. That works well in films because days, weeks, months, even years go by in very few minutes. I had only just met my Moroccan and the minutes we'd spent together were real minutes, however much I tried to change them into ellipses.

He was inviting me to his place, in some town or city. I said no, I had to work, I work at night, you know? But we must agree on a date, whatever, I need to see you again, whatever it takes. And you know, such insistence makes me lose all interest and reminds me that one day one of them will want to stay in my life forever and it will be a real bother to undo what we've done so far. I know that's so from a job I had unpicking clothes, which is much more laborious than sewing. He walked me to the station and held my hand while we waited for the train. He was laughing, jumping, saying he was so happy he had met me. It always stressed me when someone held my hand, but even more so when it was a complete stranger. What with the smell of steel from the trains on the tracks he steeled himself around my waist. When will we meet up? I don't know, I said. And the whole station went up my nose and made me feel sick. Why did he speak so sweetly? If I didn't look at him I felt he was no longer different. My love, you must think about us? My love? About us? At that point I should have run off, but I stood there quietly while his arms squeezed my body.

He kept ringing so often at all times of the day and night that on Saturday I did go to his place. A long-distance relationship, he told me, two trains to reach a station with paint flaking off its walls and half-baked graffiti on the façade. I had to wait for him because it was a station outside the town. He came late and that meant I was standing there miles from anywhere while people drove up, picked up other passengers and left me alone. It was daytime but the sky was nothing like it was the day I first met him.

I remember his small grey car and both of us going straight to his house. How come we never went to eat something? Went for a walk? Talked? I remember lots of steps. Maybe there weren't that many, but when I think about him, I can only see tenements with stairs like streets. I don't know what the town was called, only that it was close to some strange mountains that loomed above. The building itself was neither old nor new, with stairs up to his flat that were impregnated with a smell that wasn't food, rubbish, spices or perfumes. Most unpleasant. Smells annoy me when I don't know where they are coming from. Plus his smell, that started to stick on my clothes when, after he'd parked, he suddenly kissed me with a tongue that tasted strange and hands that strayed over my body bringing disorder everywhere. I reached his flat in a state and couldn't think when that nasty stuff in my nose had all started.

He shared the flat with other young men and they were still there, maybe finishing their lunch. His bedroom was one of the first along the corridor, on the right as you came in through the door. That's why we had to say hello, and then slip off furtively to his room. It was a bedroom, like the one in that painting where the furniture seems to be on the move, though more depressing because there's no colour in the picture. And because everything looked worn out, a grey blanket I imagined was from the army, a bed squeezed into one corner, a small table strewn with things, and dirty clothes everywhere. If he knew I was coming, why hadn't he at least removed the dirty clothes? Sir, don't you think men should be minimally considerate even if it's only a casual lay? He stretched me out on a spring mattress that squeaked and gave under my weight. He went on with those hands that brought disorder, that's the precise word, and hurriedly undid my blouse, his eyes changing to a dark grey and seemingly about to leap out of their sockets. He stuck his white skin inside me while I could hear the voices of other men speaking in a language I didn't recognise. Could they hear the rusty squeaking springs? Did they assume he had taken that girl into his room? Why was I so worried all of a sudden? My Moroccan thrust forcefully into me, crazily, the bed was too small and I kept hitting my head on the wall. To take my mind off that I looked at the faded brown, wrinkled socks with a hole in one corner, the white threadbare underpants, soiled down one side, the papers heaped up on folded clothes, the white walls blotched grey where paint had flaked off and exposed the cement. I felt sad I wasn't even in my own place when a bead of sweat dropped from his stifled moan onto one of my eyes; I'll tell you, in due course, how beads of sweat can sometimes be really annoying. Others, the ones you've really sought out, feel like gifts, but that wasn't the case with my Moroccan.

I don't remember how it ended. I went back once, that's for sure, because I know we strolled through a Sunday market at the foot of some cliffs that loomed above us under threatening grey clouds. I said it was late and I had to be going, you know, two trains. It must have finished like so many of my liaisons: he kept ringing and I never answered and he eventually got fed up.

the Argentinian

I went after the Argentinian because I needed him, though the few people I've told about what happened reckon he took advantage of the situation, that however much I agreed to continue our goings-on he shouldn't have started them in the first place. As it was true that I chased him, I've never blamed him, if there was a need to blame anyone, but all the same it left me with a strange aftertaste in the mouth. I still don't know if what happened was normal or not, but what is or isn't normal when it comes to sex?

I went to see him because of a mark on my skin at a time when I'd hardly started doing damage to myself. Well, it was a brownish circle under my belly that was beginning to spread. A silly little blemish, stupid to go and see a skin specialist over something like that, but you know how I was quite able to distort my reflection in the mirror in order to turn any part of me that I'd got obsessed with into something grotesque and unreal.

When I sat on the narrow bed I crossed my feet so I didn't topple off and when he was inspecting my belly, his smooth hair fell over his face and hid his eyes. He didn't smell of anything, as if he didn't exist, like that whole room that was painted white. And then there was the dark wooden frame on one side of his desk, a gadget with metal balls swinging this way and that, as if they were tick-tocking silently. Why do people have these pointless knick-knacks? So the repetitive movements distract their patients to no purpose in particular? I watched the balls that were shiny then dull while he touched the skin around my blemish with two plastic covered fingers. He was removing his glove by the time he said it wasn't anything to worry about, a little skin infection, in a singsong voice that sounded like sailing ships on the sea, their sails bobbing to and fro. When he spoke, he was everything I imagined, a vessel taking me so far away I didn't know where I was, to oceans where nothing and nobody existed. And while I pulled on my T-shirt and zipped up my trousers I could hear seagulls shrieking. Seagulls shrieking in the middle of the ocean? I'm sure they prefer to hug the coast.

When he looked up from the prescription he'd just signed he stared at me in a way that always makes me wonder, as if he was signalling something, but I've always been slow at inter- preting signals. I spot the message when I think it through later. On that occasion it was in the street, gripping that sheet of paper, when I realised his gaze had lasted a few seconds longer than necessary and that his eyes had changed colour, had veered from pale brown to dark brown, to black.

I felt that unease I always felt when I discovered a man desired me, especially when they were different. I needed to know more, exactly how much they liked me. To confirm first impressions. Obviously with the Argentinian there was the extra excitement triggered by the possibility we might meet in a place where I'd never done it, and things might happen differently. Wasn't I naive imagining that by always repeating the same scenes something different would eventually happen? The colour of the paint changed, the smells, the furniture, the skin colour, but in fact it was always a repetition of the same. I couldn't decide what to do about my niggling unease: for my peace of mind I ought to have gone back immediately, but what would have been my excuse? And what about the nurse? She must be used to it? I bet I wouldn't be the first woman he'd fucked in his consultancy, a doctor touching the skin of every body part, caring for them, protecting them, a man who knows so much about bodies with that voice like a ship in the middle of the ocean. I walked off still feeling uneasy and cursed my belated reaction.

Until we met one day in a café near his consultancy. A street corner with lots of passers-by, I remember the loud motorbikes. He was sitting by himself and when he said hello he invited me to join him, if I wasn't with anyone else, etc... He talked and talked and I laughed at his bad jokes and seized the opportunity to open my lips, take deeper breaths or gaze lingeringly into his eyes. Isn't it odd how you can imagine what a man will be like in bed before anything has actually happened? And bed meant the bed in his consultancy.

I regret I can't remember those first moments before the first kiss. You only have one first kiss with a man, you never get a repeat, just like the Englishman said. Sure, I can remember the kisses from when he'd been kissing me for awhile, the way he bit my lips with teeth as sharp as the edge of a knife. 'They're sharp!' I should have shouted out loud. I liked being bitten and felt disappointed when a man didn't dare to move on from tender nibbles to bites that sink into your skin until you lose sight of the world, but teeth always have a gentle, rounded edge however deep they dig into you, even when they were like a saw, it seemed as if they'd been filed down so they didn't cut. Not the Argentinian's, his were thin and sharp-edged, and cut deep, caused real pain, with no let up. I tried to dodge them but they went for my neck, pierced me like needles.

Sit here, he said with one hand on that narrow bed. I'd already removed my knickers and thought it wouldn't be very comfortable up there, but I obeyed. I liked to feel them leading me on, that they knew exactly what they were doing and I didn't have to take any decisions. Lie down, open your legs. More, more, and he separated out my lips to look inside, like a gynaecologist. He did that for a long time and I started to get impatient. Where was his desire if he was inspecting me like a doctor? Was something wrong down there or was he getting ready to take a lick? I didn't know whether I should be aroused by such an aseptic gaze, I didn't know how to let him know I wanted him inside me, if I'd now become an object of scrutiny. Maybe he's found one of those diseases you catch down there, maybe he didn't want to risk getting infected, maybe that infection I had further up had spread downwards. I wanted to ask him, but I said nothing all the time he was examining me. He looked at me panting for it when he said get down and jerked me round so I had my back to him, pinned to the white paper where he'd stretched me out, that was now wrinkled and torn. I remember being aroused by his unexpected move, by his hand on the back of my neck that wouldn't let me lift my head, I remember feeling completely overpowered and relieved by the unusual way he hit my buttocks and pinched my nipples that were flattened against the cold, synthetic cover. He was a good dominator who knew exactly what I wanted. How do men manage to know which woman wants to be treated like that and which doesn't? Don't think it's so easy. Maybe it's mutual recognition between dominators and women longing to be dominated?

I went back to his consultancy a couple of times, and he always followed more or less the same routine. Except I was the one who always got down on my knees and I liked to look up at him from down on the floor and see his face change as the sweat glued his hair to his temples. I liked feeling I didn't have to take any decisions, just go there and let him get on with it.

But one day he came to my place and, even though I'd unzipped his trousers in the middle of the passage to give him a blow job there and then, he insisted on going to bed for some reason. On my bed without a head rest I thought my Argentinian suddenly seemed at a loss and was as clumsy as the other men who'd passed that way, just one more awkward adolescent. I thought he'd performed very expertly in his consultancy, his territory. That day he didn't get his usual erection and maybe that's why I never returned any of his calls. Or maybe because however much I sniffed the inside of his elbows and armpits I never found any smell at all.

the Lebanese guy

Things always happen on trains, you know all about that. All the more so when you're on your way home and the day's ending without a body in sight and you feel loneliness wrenching both sides of your throat. The carriages were half empty the day I met the Lebanese guy, it was late on Saturday. I sat down and wriggled my feet out of my sandals and parked them on the seat, my ankles threatening to knot together as usual. I'm not sure whether I was feeling relieved I'd not picked a man up on that journey. I'd remember others, when I was alone, they'd pass over me, one after another, like waves. I was into that when the Lebanese guy sat next to my feet, and he gave off the cloying scent of a perfume I didn't recognize, that didn't let me catch a smell of him. A few days later, in my place, he showed me a pill he said he always carried in his pocket: musk, he said, they get it from *los cojones* of some animal.

He started to talk about the weather, the landscape, life, as if it was an everyday situation, as if we were just two passengers sharing a space, as if my legs weren't so close to him, as if desire hadn't sparked off some of his ever so casual words in Spanish. Wouldn't it be nice to spend a night under the stars with incense and lute music, candles and delicious Arab food? Pastries and mint tea? Wouldn't it be nice if you and I were sitting on silk cushions listening to nice songs? I didn't laugh. I found it sickening to imagine so many smells all at once, and his jeans hardly fitted such a scene. Was it his strategy for seduction? Maybe he'd met other women like me who are crazy about meeting somebody different and was making the most of his difference? I opened my eyes wide in surprise and tried to laugh. Don't you like romance? No. I told him not that kind, because at the time I was thinking how I hated any kind of romanticising; I didn't tell him I preferred to imagine my own scenarios in distant, exotic countries and didn't want my men with a difference telling me, because that took all the fun away.

He suddenly started to sing, making strange sounds, over-acting expressions of suffering, pain, pleasure or whatever, because I couldn't understand the words. He grabbed one of my feet when I angrily tried to change seats, the one that had been pressing the other down for some time, and began to massage the sole. I watched the trees rushing past, the small hills I could intuit in the dark because I was familiar with the route, the factories that were lit up and the houses with sloping roofs, all to avoid looking at him. I didn't until later when he'd been running his fingers from my heel to my instep and I leant my head back oblivious to where I was or what I was doing there. I don't imagine you think it very normal for a strange man to be massaging my feet in a train, but at the time I didn't find it at all odd, simply exciting. I only looked up in surprise when I felt they wrenched something inside me, unexpectedly. That was the moment my Lebanese guy hit the spot he had hit once and had been looking for ever since because he knew that when he pressed it I would be lost to the world, it was the trigger. The Lebanese guy realized that, that spot on the sole of my foot had given me the shudders: it was then I looked into his eyes, I'm not sure whether I was frightened or defiant. He didn't stop until I looked overwhelmed, until I smiled gleefully at him. I want something in exchange. What? You wearing knickers or a thong? A thong. I want you to go to the lavatory, take it off and give it to me.

I came straight back. My knickers were wet and he kept sniffing them. In my country I was an army lieutenant for a long time. Shut up, I was thinking, I couldn't get my head around his story, couldn't imagine the scenery, moons, suns, anything. But there was no stopping him from filling me in on the details of the town where he grew up, the place where he studied, his family, all exotically sugary-sweet – that wasn't what I was after when I was with one of my guys with a difference. That's why I suggested we should go to the lavatory. That's why I let his bites go deeper than the others and discovered I could tolerate even more pain, that when teeth slightly penetrate your skin the pain quickly veers into the most intense pleasure. There was a puddle of water and piss on the lavatory floor, and the paper hanging from the dispenser was soaked half way up because of the to and fro of the train. It wasn't comfortable, pleasant or pleasurable. And much less so with that stained mirror where I could see myself looking as if I was putting up with pain but didn't know where it was really coming from or at what rate. He squeezed my nipples, grabbed my hair and pulled it back until I couldn't move if I didn't want to feel the roots tighten and threaten to depart my skull. It was sudden and violent, nothing like his tale of candles and lutes. Do men like sex like that, grabbing you, not letting go and dominating you? Did I like sex in train lavatories covered in piss and teeth digging in and tearing the skin on my neck quite at will? He pulled my hair even tighter behind me and I felt like screaming but neither of us opened our mouths so we wouldn't be heard. My neck was pulled taut and my mouth crushed. And now I knew what it was like to lose total control of your body, I saw myself as more animal-like than ever, surrendering to my predator, who could have beheaded me on the spot if he'd wanted, or easily strangled me if he'd wanted. It was total surrender and maybe it was seeing how much I was enjoying the ride in the mirror that scared me and made me wonder if that's what I'd be doing from then on and if I'd be satisfied with a few bites and squeezes or would ask for something stronger. I'm not sure whether you can imagine the dizziness you feel when you reach your own limits and go beyond them, a sort of euphoria in the abyss.

The Lebanese guy had to get out one stop before me and he asked to meet up again. He came to my place just once. He was more restless than in the train, very nervous, and lost the plot with my body, didn't know what to do next. He didn't linger on my neck at all and I couldn't help feeling disappointed. A few kisses and bites, but he didn't half-strangle me or wrench my head backwards as if he was going to break my neck. He was more into mauling my breasts and seemed to want to slot his member in my mouth but I was long past wanting any of that. I didn't even register when he stuck it inside me: I was annoyed, but I'm not sure whether it was his size or because I'd stretched so. At the time I thought I'd stretched more than is normal because I'd taken so many men and would never go back to my previous size. I came with great difficulty, was still panting on one side of the bed, when I got a card out of my bag. What's that? The night-bus timetable. Sure, he was livid, but by that time if I couldn't even stand the sight of myself, I felt even less like having him by my side all night and waking up to see him asleep there in the morning.

the Basque

I've met some men by day as the light spread over their skin. Yes, I know I've told you about encounters with lovers in the midday sun, but they don't count if I was working at night because in fact night is day as far as I go. Is that difficult to understand? It's not, it's really easy: when I've spent the night in the factory what I see in daylight hours is ersatz life. You, sir, see me here and think I'm here, awake, but it's an illusion. The only way I've found to feel as if I was experiencing real life was the holidays. Yes, it's obvious that everyone refuels in the holidays, but for us people who work nights those few weeks when we sleep at the proper time it's like being born again. That's why I remember what happened to me with the Basque as being different from my experiences with other men. Right, I know I'm always telling you that it is different, but I tell you that in this case it was true. It isn't just one of my crazy notions that keeps changing and getting clearer as time goes by. No, for a start I met the Basque on a beach one day when I was sunbathing on a towel. As you can imagine, near a huge stretch of water. You see, I've not met all my lovers on trains. He was lying next to me and it was some time before I realized he was gazing at me. It was a day of shouting, shivering and splashing, with people lifting their arms up when they were half in the water, and plastic spades hitting the compact sand that had slurped out of buckets. I could hear all that when I realized that he was staring at me from his towel and, believe me, it's never the same if they stare at you standing or sitting down, as when their bodies are sprawled over the ground. That day we were both on our fronts, our lust racing on unleashed. People don't usually give any importance to this kind of thing, they often say it doesn't matter what pose you're striking when they meet you, but, believe me, it is important. The fact is we normally meet people standing up. Besides, it was sticky, boiling hot and the sun was blistering down on our backs. Seen from the outside, in parallel, on rough towels that had seen other summers, nobody would have noticed any excitement, anything unusual for a beach. We were stretched out for a good while staring into each other's eyes. Had I gone to the beach with anyone? Yes, some girlfriends or workmates who were maybe next to me and as motionless as I was, and that's why they didn't see the fireworks sparking across centi-metres of sand. Yes, 'fireworks' was the word, you must know how reactions between bodies are automatic, biological and primitive. Bodies are attracted to each other by something aside from whatever we do, by an invisible particle bringing them together. We often ignore the animal discharges pushing us in the direction of someone, but you know at the time I never missed out on one. I wanted to know what was behind all the mutual attraction, what the universe wanted to tell me with that reaction I could only understand as being chemical. At any rate, I was convinced there must be a good reason for certain things to happen. Or worse even, that my prurient conscience played no part. It was powered by sudden adrenalin-driven excitement. I suppose it's not surprising with such a short-lived surge if I've forgotten which summer it was or the name of the Basque, that is, if we ever got that far. I do remember that he was a big, big body and face, with red-striped white skin and a freckled back. I remember his freckles vividly, I could draw them, and the patch of reddish white skin separating them, could draw the map of that from memory in the same way I could repeat the Ghanaian's mysterious litany. Don't you think it's peculiar the way I retain this kind of trivial detail?

I sometimes think there should be adventures that freeze at that initial point when we know we are two complete strangers and look at each other trying to guess what the other is thinking. The Basque's big, ill-assorted teeth immediately led me to imagine a sexual mayhem of wild, fast and furious bites though maybe not as much as I later encountered. I've already talked, sir, about the possibility of intuiting men's character in bed. At the time I thought it was a fascinating, almost esoteric skill.

We said next to nothing before walking to his flat. Did I say goodbye to the people I was with, did they look surprised, thrilled or disapproving? Did they say you must be mad, or ring right away, if he gives you grief? Sure they saw dangers I never saw. But at the time I reckoned that, in fact, I was risking nothing, sure as I was that whatever might happen, one way or the other, would end up being very exciting and an addition to my collection of exotic encounters.

I don't remember a single kiss. It's not a case of memory loss: there weren't any. And you bet, I'd have liked a few, judging by his teeth that seemed to want to fly out of his mouth, his large, angular face and bushy eyebrows. I was thinking of green mountains, of big trees cut by an axe. I was thinking silently about axes and forests when he beat me across the buttocks with his flat hand the second we walked into his place. It surprised me because it was different to the way I'd been smacked by other men, whether playfully or with more serious intent. Others were like tentative explorers, as if they didn't know if that was really what I wanted them to do and gave me quizzical looks until they could see the road was clear. However, the Basque never asked permission to beat me and was completely confident about what he was doing. His was a carefully calculated, expert slap. I thought that maybe he was more skilled than I was at guessing the sexual personalities of women and felt quite stressed that I was so transparent. All his slaps followed the precise surgical line of the first. He lifted his hand really high before crashing it down on my flesh, bringing pain that was searing at first and then left my skin feeling itchy and sore. I felt blood rush there straightaway, crying out for relief. I tried to lower a hand to soothe the sting, but he held me tight by the wrists. I then received another onslaught that electrified exactly the same spot. He said virtually nothing, only asked me now and then whether I wanted more. I looked defiant and said I did, harder, much harder. You sure? You sure you can take it? Then he lifted his hand even higher, hoping I would give him the nod.

I don't remember my Basque ever embracing me, though

when I think about it I can't stop that flow of warm emotion that comes when you recall long, conventional relationships, Sundays spent at the cinema, leisurely strolls on a Saturday afternoon and planning holidays together. It must be because he made his mark on me from head to toe, and I can still trace him on my body. The bites on the shoulder while he was beating my bum, from teeth that tested the elasticity of my skin to the limit, that provoked intense pain and threatened to make me lose consciousness at any moment. But the pain immediately gave way to a feeling of lightness, as if I was floating pleasurably and had left my battered, disfigured body mass exhausted and floppy on a chair. A pause. When the Basque tired of my bum he spun me round so I was facing him and started hitting my breasts, something a man had never done to me before, whether hard or lightly. Breasts are soft, delicate flesh that doesn't tolerate being squeezed, and, what's more, difficult to hit, don't offer the same expanse as buttocks. But the Basque knew what he was about and lifted his hand and let it fall like the lash of a whip, skilfully so as to hit only the upper part and not touch the nipple. I glanced across the wicker sofa and glass-topped table; the skin that hadn't tanned was going red and I could make out separate blue patches forming that would eventually merge into one big blotch. He started twisting my nipple until I thought it would drop off. More? I always said more, out of pride and because I wanted more. It's strange how I felt total bliss, the supreme expression of freedom in the sublimation of that pain. Sick, right? But I didn't think so at the time, I was thinking that was exactly what I'd decided I wanted, so nobody could say it wasn't a good thing.

He went on and on. To tell you the truth, though he was giving me lots of pleasure, I was hoping it would be foreplay, that we'd then end up as you always do, but he didn't want to. He was still beating me when he started to masturbate in front of me and splashed his cum all over me, also in a very calculated way. Maybe I'd have got angry in another place or time, maybe I'd have felt cheated, but I was immensely grateful that someone had finally made my body seem so alien, I felt my skin so taut, so on fire everywhere, that I didn't protest. I left feeling satisfied in a strange kind of way. And with one nagging doubt: what if I couldn't live without all that from now on, if I needed nothing less for a good fuck? How would men react when I said beat me, whip me, squeeze me?

Virtual Man

Computers have never appealed to me, let alone finding men on the Internet. In fact, to tell you the truth, I held out against what they call new technologies as long as I could. As they were never any use in my work I dodged as best I could every opportunity to use a computer. When I was at secondary school those of us who used typewriters were still in the majority. But then everywhere was suddenly flooded with those machines and even cleaning ladies started to surf the web. I don't know what happened but I woke up one morning and everyone had a computer. It was quite crazy! And so many women dating men on the Internet! Some even married them. I still haven't got to the bottom of it although I have been shown how to use a web-cam. There are ladies working at the factory who, two days after learning to use a mouse, spend the whole day talking to strangers. As far as I'm concerned if I can't smell a man from the start, I can't tell whether he interests me or not. However, you have to try your hand at everything going, and though I was extremely reluctant, I did get into a conversation with a man I couldn't see. I was in the house of a friend who taught me how to chat. She showed me the steps to take, how to invent a stupid name I don't remember and then wait for something to happen. Sentences in different colours started to pop up that made me want to vomit. Everyone was speaking to everyone else. Did they know each other? Were they friends and was I the last one on the block? It was all good humoured and polite, with strange names that seemed to belong nowhere, letters mixed up with numbers, signs that meant nothing to me. I got into a state at the start and couldn't cope with all the messages. Until they began to say hello, where are you from and what do you do? Who were they? So many people connected to the Internet all day that I could never get to know.

One name caught my eye, the name of someone I thought must be different. He quickly invited me into a private chat room. What on earth is a private chat room? I followed his instructions until I was in a conversation with him alone. He asked me what I was like and I recalled tawdry moments with tacky men slavering at the other end of the line as their heavy voices asked me to give a detailed description of myself. What colour hair, eyes, how tall, how much did I weigh, and not to get angry if he asked me a question. No, sure I wouldn't get angry. Dead sure. What size bra do you wear? As if that revealed anything about my breasts apart from size, as if it told you what they were like to touch, whether they were soft, whether they drooped, were sad or optimistic, had thin or broad, brown or pink aureoles, little or big nipples. My bra size was simply that as far as I was concerned, what I needed to go into a shop and say I wanted this size or that. But the guy started to send me all kinds of little drawings after I told him my size. And exclamation marks! And what about transferring to Messenger? Will you give me your address? Will you accept me? My head was spinning with all those things I saw as pointless and perhaps that was why I started breathing faster.

I made him wait while I set up an account, learned how to start up, and how it worked. And he began to ask things like what do you like people doing to you. I found it exciting not being able to see his face, not knowing who he was, whether he'd reject me, I'd reject him, he'd repel or scare me, or whatever. I found it exciting only having his words, even though they sometimes sounded hackneyed, copied from the telly, like what are you wearing now. And obviously, I couldn't be wearing the striped pyjamas my girlfriend had lent me or a turban round my head to gather my hair up before going to bed or be with her watching a series while she ate bacon twists and poked a finger in her ear. No, better to be naked, clad only in a silk dressing gown with wide sleeves, though I hadn't a clue why they had to be wide. Now we started to play at saying what we would like to do to each other, and what we *would* do to each other. First I'd take off your dressing gown and nibble and lick you all over. So predictable, I thought, and I waited for him to ask me to tell him what I really wanted, something I'd never say to a man I could smell because when I'm with men I can smell I do everything without saying a word, they know what I want without my having to spell it out. I like being hit. And hard. Until I'm black and blue. Would you do that? You bet I would, and use a whip, on your buttocks, wherever you wanted it. And if you like, I'll put a dog collar on you and take you for a walk while I hit you. And I'll tie your hands and feet up so you can't move unless I let you, and I'll beat you on your bum till you bleed. You scared of blood? There are lots of pansies around who say they like the rod and then faint at the sight of a drop of blood. Has anyone ever made you bleed? Has anyone ripped out a piece of your skin with his teeth? No, never. I'd love you to come and do that to me. And writing that was like when you ride a ghost train at the fairground and let out a blood-curdling scream to get rid of your fear, long before you've even seen your first ghost. You'll come and see me and you'll be my little dog. What do you reckon? Will you? You must wear a mini-skirt and no knickers and I'll take you to every bar in my city, on a tight leash with your bum in the air so everyone can have a good look. What else do you want me to do? Do you want me to whack your behind? Wallop it till it bleeds? Are you up for that? Yes, I really am. A real little tart, right? To tell you the truth, however much he qualified that word with 'little', the vibrations round his words suggested he felt only contempt for women, way beyond the tinny words used in this kind of game. He kept repeating, will you come? making all those meaningful pauses. Hey, will you come and see me? What else do you want me to do to you? Do you want to try it with another girl? No, I don't like that. So, what do you like? With another man? See, you are a real little tart. I promise you, if you come, I'll take you everywhere dripping wet and at the end of the night I'll get a lad who'll be good for both of us, you just come. Mind you, I won't let you go until you're good and satisfied, until your body is black and blue and we've both fucked you everywhere and you're begging us to stop. And do you know what we'll do right at the end? Do you know what we'll finish on? When you're on the ground, with the dog collar on, all black and blue, and looking at us and saying please, I've had enough, when you can't stand any more, we'll both piss on you. And our hot piss will splash on your face and you will love it.

Right then, as if I'd been jolted in a bus, I snapped out of that screen hypnosis, from that strange, honestly unsettling need to find out what that man was like, what stuff his fantasies were made of and how far he wanted to go. I looked at my girl-friend sitting there half asleep, as if everything around me was a thousand kilometres away. I had never thought that I really wanted to do what I'd said I wanted, but Virtual Man kept insisting on sorting the details for me to go and see him. It was so easy, so at hand. Just fix a day and time and he'd pick me up at the station. He sent me a photo: a man past forty with hair dyed blond. A photo that revealed nothing. Suddenly it was one big challenge, would I dare do all that? So what if I don't know the area and it's only a one-off? If nobody there knows me, why can't I go half naked and arouse all the men around? And lie between two bodies, and get beaten until I lose sight of my body, and I cease to be myself? I was frightened, not by them, but by the thought I'd not know when to stop, and then would never go with a man who didn't do all that kind of thing. If I did fall in love with a man one day, would he want to piss on me when he eventually found out that was what I craved? Why was I so taken with such an insulting image of myself? Was it a punishment? For which sin in particular? Like they say happens when you die, I saw a rapid succession of images of my lovers, as if I was in an endless race. I got really upset when I discovered I couldn't decide the exact moment I stopped walking peacefully along and started to race before breaking into a sprint. For the first time in my life I wondered who was chasing me. Even so, as you know, I still took quite a time to come to a halt.

As far as Virtual Man is concerned, fear brought me to a halt in the station for long distance trains. Yes, I tell you I did really feel scared, I couldn't say whether it was by what might await me at the end of the ride or by the idea that I might cross an invisible line that would forever deprive me of the chance of aspiring to sex that deals in caresses, kisses and tenderness. As you can imagine, at the time I couldn't have expressed it like that. As I stood on the station platform the stench of piss hit me from all those shabby lavatory stalls where I'd fucked total strangers.

the Chinaman

My affair with the Chinaman was a surprise extra. Not because I'd decided to cut back on the number of strange bodies encountering mine, but because exhaustion led me to live mechanically, from day to day, rather than in a way I really wanted. I'd transformed myself into a stranger, like all those guys. I was getting more and more like my lovers. On the other hand, you know, what happened with the Chinaman had its funny side. Its sad side too. Predictably, I met the Chinaman in a restaurant. I'd like to think I'd seen him round and about, shuffling down the street, or that I'd bumped into him in the neighbourhood, but I hadn't. He came over to talk to me because he was astonished I was dining out alone. I've told you how I often ate alone in restaurants because I couldn't be bothered to ring anyone. He told me he owned the place, in fact owned a number of restaurants, and that his son was learning to cook, they were extending their range and he now did Japanese cuisine too, as it was so fashionable. He brought me a strange little roll to try with a green sauce, that I had to swallow in one gulp. He piled the sauce on. When it was in my mouth I thought it tasted horrible and I couldn't get it down, it was hot in a way I didn't recognize that made me feel queasy, but he'd already sat down and was pouring me wine as if it was water. I choked down the feeling I was about to vomit while beads of sweat streamed down my forehead and I tried to chew without really tasting the flavours, imagining how I'd panic when the time came to swallow the ball in my mouth. Couldn't I disappear for a moment and get rid of it? No, my Chinaman wouldn't go, he just kept telling me to drink and I obeyed, trying to dilute the green sauce with red wine. It was worse when I swallowed the lot at one go: the aftertaste wouldn't go away. I kept drinking. He got up, sat next to me and poured me more wine, rubbing against one of my breasts as if by chance. He repeated the move, the same gesture while I think he looked me in the eye, intensely. I say intensely because I found it difficult to gauge how such little eyes were gazing at me.

That's why I had never liked Chinamen, even though they are so different. I didn't like the way they walked up and down, looked without seeming to, and I didn't like a smell that took me nowhere. To Africa, the Orient, or days when it was bright and sunny or poured with rain. I didn't know what to imagine with Chinamen. Yes, I know, there should have been lots, vast, misty landscapes with mountains divided up by walls, but they didn't appeal to my imagination like men from other countries.

So I didn't know *what* to imagine with my Chinaman when I got into his car and he immediately put his hand on my thigh. He was small, very small and I thought he'd be tacky and slippery. I thought we'd go to a hotel; it was one of those cars with light coloured, reclining leather seats. We drove alongside the river, to a spot under a bridge where cars sped by at top speed. A depressing place littered with used condoms and other cars parked all around, a place for adolescents or people with nowhere else to go. What was I doing there with an unknown Chinaman whose fingers were feeling me up? Why didn't his smell trigger any scenes in my mind, why couldn't I imagine him far from there, far from me? He didn't look at me, he disgusted me, or I disgusted myself when he looked at my sad face in the rear-view mirror. I grabbed his fingers and pointed them to where he wanted to go. He rolled them to and fro quickly, still on mine that were guiding him and I came in no time. Now me, missee, he said, now me, missee, and when I said no, I felt very sad. As if I'd suddenly become a different kind of human, joined a species unable to feel any kind of empathy with others. I wanted to punish him, you know, not so much to punish him as an individual with those specific traits there and then with me as to punish men everywhere.

I got out of the car to avoid seeing him or hearing him say, now me, missee. I walked home as best I could, as if I was walking in the dark. I don't remember how I got to sleep.

Nowhere Man

When I met Nowhere Man I didn't know he would be the last
of this kind of man I'd go out with, that he'd be the last I'd
be tempted to fuck for fucking's sake. Well, he wasn't quite
the last, but the last I wanted, before I learned what I learned
from you, sir. You know the change didn't happen overnight,
I didn't wake up one day and realise I couldn't go on with that
style of life. The women at work were already saying that the
moment comes when you grow up and get some commonsense,
but they wouldn't have said it in so many words. They say that
as if it was a question of age and that's not true, it's more about
how much you want it or knowing exactly what you want and
don't want. Maybe you, sir, would say we know what we want
at each stage, but that's not true, it takes a lifetime to know
what we like and what we don't. Nowhere Man was simultaneously man and woman. I call him Nowhere Man because
he never told me where he came from, he refused to, said why
does that matter, repeatedly, as he gripped one elbow with his
hand and rested his chin on the inside of the other. They are
the kind of questions people should learn not to ask, who you
are, where you are from, where you were born are matters of
chance. As is the sex you're born with, male or female. Don't

you agree? But I noticed he had a different accent and so I continued the conversation that day when he sat next to me in a station where lots of people were hustling and bustling. A man with shortish hair who didn't dress like a woman but said he was one. That's how the conversation began, with he/she asking me to buy a packet of paper hankies from him. Oh, thank you, darling, thank you so much. You don't know how difficult it is to get people to respect you just a little bit. What harm am I doing anyone? I'm only selling tissues, if they want them, and it's fine if they don't. But a lot of men get angry just because I speak to them, even if it's just one word. Isn't that odd? It was then when that bright shining trust was sealed between us that he sat down on a grey, cold plastic bench. Know what? I do this because I don't have any choice, because I can't do anything else. I can't work in a normal job, they look at my ID and see what my name really is and think I'm odd … I've not changed that much, I don't like transsexuals who change themselves into whores rather than women. Have you ever noticed that? They give themselves huge boobs and fill their lips with silicone and end up making a caricature of themselves. Not me, I prefer to be myself and for everyone to see clearly that I am a woman, and I need to change hardly anything to manage that. It's a matter of attitude. You're a woman if you want to be a woman, no need to make life complicated. I can tell you that there are a hell of a lot of women with fantastic breasts and bums who don't want to be women. While he/she spoke, people walked past and trains made a din that annoyed me when they hurtled down the tracks. As for me, I just need to remove one thing, right? And he looked at his crossed thighs and put a hand on my shoulder. I'm saving up for the operation and will soon have enough. I'll get rid of that nuisance down there. And he laughed with a lady's voice, an old dearie's voice. He/she kept getting nearer and nearer, nearer and nearer, and while he talked, he touched my knee, my arm and occasionally a lock of hair. Listen, you seem like a really nice person, he said. Do you like pretty underwear? I said I did and he/she asked what I was wearing then. I told him I couldn't remember, maybe it was purple. Hmmm, I bet it's a really lovely bra, you can see from the way they look. They must be really lovely. Will you let me have a look? As I didn't know whether he/she was male or female, I found the question disconcerting. If it had been a woman who'd been born a woman who had sat next to me in a train station and asked to see my bra, would I have said yes? No, I'm sure I wouldn't. But it was different with him/her and I flashed a strap at him. It's lovely, really lovely. Can I touch it? And he/she touched it a good long while until finally he/she slipped his/her hand down inside, on the sly, and gently fondled one of my breasts. I think yours must be so lovely, such firm flesh that will never sag. He/she looked at me as men do when they have the hots for you. Won't you let me have a look? and his hand was still on me. Imagine how exciting it was. That he was a she who liked me, and was fondling my breast in the middle of that crowd and suggesting I go with him. There are places in the station where you can get peace and quiet, won't you come with me? I was still looking at him rather taken aback when I said but you are a woman in a man's body, aren't you? Sure, sweetie, but I'm a lesbie.

From time to time I still see him stopping to talk to somebody and I think he doesn't recognise me, that what he did with me he must do with others, whether men or women. I said no, it was getting late, that I'd be late for work. I didn't want to find out what his secret was. Or get to know his desire or any other man's desire. Because behind all the mystery there's only misfortune, a mishap or defect. Though, of course, maybe it's just that I'm tired of flawed men, of disturbed, bad-tempered, alcoholic, impotent or pathetic men. Men as flawed as I am.

TWO ILLUSIONS

you, sir

She's on the kitchen floor, on all fours, knees in trousers so they don't get in the way. She's gathered up her hair, barely held in place by a clip, revealing the nape of her neck that's now beginning to glisten with sweat. If you look carefully you can count her heartbeats by the pace at which her blood courses through the veins of her tensed neck, interrupted now and then when she suddenly swallows down saliva. Her mouth's half-open and she hasn't noticed how her breathing has quickened into a gentle pant. A trickle of shiny saliva threatens to slip through the gap shaped by her lower lip and teeth and fall on the floor tiles, but, ever on the alert, she eagerly sucks it back in and swallows it down, biting the inside of her cheek in the process. A lock of hair separates out and drops on her moist shoulders. Very soon, another falls over her collarbone. Her whole body pushes forward from the back, each wipe brings an imperceptible increase in pressure on the ground, her knuckles blanching whenever her fists close tight. Her posture underlines the curve of her back, her prominent buttocks, creating a sudden descent to the depths of her waist until, further up, her back emerges, sinewy muscle rippling under skin padded by a thin layer of fat. Her knees push hard against the floor, begin to hurt, threaten to go dead for a while. She moves one, then the next, so they hold up until she is finished. She wouldn't normally have worked like that, but she'd decided she ought to put in a bigger effort on what was her first day. The underwire of her bra cuts into her, the softest part of her breasts rubbing against it with each wipe she makes, but she hasn't time to take it off, it's too late. She yanks it down now and then, is horrified by the thought of the marks it leaves, the dark brown circles where her armpit starts. But her real unease stems from the threat they might escape altogether: her breasts appear to have a mind of their own when she is in this position, as if they no longer belong to her anatomy. She has gradually accelerated her actions to finish the job quickly, and her cheeks have turned a dark red, small beads of sweat now drip on the ground. She is also breathing faster and heavier.

Forward and back, forward and back, putting her whole body into it until she's finished and rocks on her heels. Brush in one hand, she tries to wipe her forehead on the stretch of arm not covered by the plastic glove that is spraying fine dust over her skin.

You see, here I can assure you that I felt satisfied. At that exact moment, after unleashing all my strength on the tiles, through my hands, my arms, my whole back, after feeling that every muscle in my body had joined in the task of making that corner of the world a little cleaner, I felt I had rid myself of a useless burden.

The writer got up from his chair, his curiosity aroused by the sounds coming out of the kitchen. He is upset in a way he can't fathom by the less than noisy manner the new cleaning lady goes about her work, and he is a man who had never wanted one because he was worried about losing his privacy. Nonetheless, in recent times, driven by an apathy that seemed to dominate his writing as well as the rest of his existence, he'd decided to take notice of his friends who also belong to the world of books and had asked the lady who cleaned for them all. However, she was fully booked and recommended a friend, an ex-colleague in another job, who could be trusted one hundred per cent. Some time ago he'd opened his door to a girl who seemed far too young for this kind of work. Perhaps she was a foreigner? No, when he spoke to her, he'd seen she wasn't from abroad. Perhaps she was a student paying her fees with a few hours' work, though they usually worked as shop assistants or on supermarket checkouts. What if she were a spy? A journalist in disguise writing a report on the way he writes? The writer soon halts that train of thought and sadly reminds himself that his reputation doesn't stretch that far. His relationship with her had begun with the mysteries surrounding her age and provenance. What's a girl like you doing in a place like this? As it was the first time they'd met he'd not dared to ask how come she spent her time cleaning other people's houses when she could have done almost anything else with her life, the girl would have taken fright and mistaken him for a dirty old man who wants to save her from poverty in pure *Pretty Woman* manner, and probably better not to risk that if you don't have the good looks of a Richard Gere. He thinks that all in good time, things must be said at the right time if you don't want to trigger the wrong reaction in the person listening to you. The writer has this special ability that makes it easier for him to pursue his trade: knowing how to wait for exactly the right moment to say what has to be said, neither too late, nor too soon. Rather than making a comment, he arched his eyebrows and ushered her in. When she said his name she thought it was a nice name for a pair of such sooty eyes, but she too refrained from making any comment. And a pleasant hand to touch given they were his work tools, but she kept quiet. He told her that nobody had ever cleaned his flat before, that she only need do four essential things to keep on top of it, dust, sweep, wash the floors and clean the lavatories, and clean the windows and kitchen every once in a while. There was no need to iron or see to his clothes, because he liked to do that. Four hours once a week.

The day I started in his house I didn't know exactly what I was doing there. Yes, of course, a little overtime to earn a pittance, but in retrospect I think it really brought me something else. If I told him that, he would laugh, if I told him that the moment I entered his flat, I felt I was entering a different place to anywhere I'd been before. I find it hard to remember that time in my life, but I do remember the feeling of peace I experienced there. Maybe because you, sir, live in that remote alley and very rarely hear anything except for the sound of a neighbour's high heels. I couldn't say. It's only now, when I think back, and think of myself standing there on your doorstep that I feel sadly nostalgic for the woman I was then. Isn't it foolish to shed tears over oneself?

You will say it isn't, that feelings are never foolish. I don't know why I find that woman on your doorstep so upsetting. Maybe she was more dead than alive. Look at me now, crying like some simple soul.

He's now standing in the kitchen doorway, looking at her. Not spying, observing, which is what a good novelist does, and silently. What are you doing cleaning the floor on your knees like women in the old days? You've got a new sweeping broom that I bought only yesterday, and all those other cleaning products. The green, yellow and blue ones. Rather than interrupt her, he prefers to follow her movements for a while. She puts all her body into it, brings the brush down on the tiles with all her might, her fingers keeping a tight hold on the small piece of wood with bristles. Are the tiles that dirty? He could act as if to clear his throat, so she knows he's there, say something or other to alert her to her new situation as a woman under observation. Right, under observation because he's a writer with a recognised track record who is continuously scrutinising the reality around him so he can reflect it in novels that will become documents that are highly prized by future generations who want to know about times past. He laughs silently imagining himself coming out loud with such a grandiloquent statement. The writer isn't looking at her just for the sake of it, on a whim, or even out of curiosity provoked by the sight of a woman, whose flesh is still firm, on all fours on a kitchen floor where no woman has been for some time. His interest is purely professional, really, no irony intended.

Listen, perhaps you don't need to clean the floor like that, you could use this. With the soles of her fleet flattened by her whole body weight and her tendons stretched to the limit, she looks round in dismay at the writer standing there, whom she hadn't noticed until then. She knocks a wisp of hair from her forehead with the inside of her elbow and shakes her head. A broom will never shift that dirt, it will only go like this, with a good stiff brush. But I'm really sorry you have to do it on your knees...Don't worry, I'll only do it this once. People think the black stuff between the tiles is natural, that tilers leave it like that because it is pretty, but just take a look. The cracks are white, when they've laid the tiles, they apply a white paste, a white wash, that we women in the cleaning gang then have to polish. And if they don't use that paste, the lines are grey. Grey or white, but never black, never like yours, extending from one corner of a tile to the next. I never noticed. No, no one notices these things, but can't you see how the floor looks newer now? The writer surveys his floor rather shamefaced, unable to believe there could have been so much dirt in what he'd thought was just one more feature in the rectangular patterning of his kitchen. Do you clean any other houses apart from mine? he asked, diverting the conversation away from an excessive focus on him and his dirt. No, yours is the first, sir; I have always worked for a company, a factory and sometimes a cleaning gang, you know, new buildings, offices, shops, stores and other premises. I prefer the factory, because I earn more money on the night shift and the work is always in the same place, and whatever the production line, the machines are all the same. You mean you work nights? Almost always. The writer goes quiet, absentmindedly scratches his head and turns to his desk. He types away while he listens to her still busying herself in his kitchen, emerging with a bucket full of tools and liquids on her way to the bathroom. He's typing but not writing anything, he is roaming the web as usual when he loses concentration. Writing requires isolation that doesn't embrace a young woman walking round the house, he doesn't want to hear her coming and going and making noise in his flat, it's a process too private to carry out in the presence of strangers. He again wonders whether she might be a journalist disguised as a cleaner. Nobody has ever seen him write, nobody has ever watched him while he concentrated on finishing a chapter or turned over an initial idea – though, to be sure, nothing could be more tedious than the sight of a writer writing, however fascinating some readers might find it. It's hardly like a surgeon operating or a chef creating his signature dish. A writer is simply a man in front of a computer. He's now completely lost the thread of what he was narrating and goes for a stroll.

he

Her thighs press hard against the bottom of the window. When she bends her knees, her damp skin rubs for a second against the cold glass. Her faded dark blue overall, with invisible stitching on the hem, rides up, glancing against the surface as it falls, leaving marks that quickly disappear. She's not wearing shoes. When the material concertinas, it threatens to reveal her knickers, but only threatens. When her toes flex hard against the ground as if she's ready to take off, her whole body tenses like a rope that spans the whole height of the window. It's the tension of orgasm, the whole body contracting before the moment of complete surrender. But she repeats the move every second, rises up and down, toes firmly on the ground, never losing contact. When she moves an arm, her shoulder blades meld and form one long, gleaming depression. The skin round her elbow thickens into a patch that's never really pink or grey. She releases tension with a deep rush of air from her throat, across her tongue and lips, and declares the job finished.

I remember very clearly the day when I first cleaned your windows. You won't believe this but the first time I clean something it becomes etched on my mind forever. No, I'm not exaggerating. You've been living in this house for a long time, but I bet you remember lots of detail from the first day as if it was yesterday. Well, I can tell you exactly what I was thinking, what images passed through my mind with every wipe of the cloth as I worked my arm that day as quickly as I could to avoid leaving any trace. Images I tried to erase just as I tried to erase those stubborn circles on the window panes. Wiping time and again.

I was thinking about Him, who always came when He shouldn't. He had just sent a text message though my mobile was in silent mode. But that didn't prevent Him from stirring me from fantasies of hoses, disinfectant and scattered scraps of ham and cheese. I was dreaming that somebody rang the bell when the bell rang, the dream was perhaps simply a reflection of the real sound, the bell somebody had been ringing for a time though I didn't wake up until the sound entered my dreams. I clung to the sheets and pulled them up to my chin. They felt warm. When you sleep during the day you are always hot when you wake up, like when you are ill. Daytime sleep is not real sleep, I've always thought they should invent another verb. I shut my eyes and returned to the water now spurting with morsels of what? Olives? Mushrooms? Nonetheless, whoever was ringing wasn't going to go away and disrupted the concentration I needed to reproduce what I'd been feeling before I'd been interrupted. I soon realised it must be Him, people who distribute advertising stuff were never so patient.

You see, I went to the door planning to express my indignation in the rudest way possible. I was going to shout 'I've told you a thousand times not to come at this time of day. Who the hell do you think you are? Fuck off, for Christ's sake!' but as you can imagine the moment I opened the door all my annoyance evaporated. I'm not sure if it was because I couldn't be bothered or because I'd seen his nervous, excited grin. You could see He was excited from the way He kept looking this way and that quite at a loss, even if that was typical of how He behaved towards me, I don't know if He was any different with other people. He only seemed to calm down for a few minutes after orgasm. As it was so inevitable that it would be Him, I turned round to go back to bed with a sigh of resignation, leaving the door ajar, but before my body could set off down the passageway, He grabbed my wrist. Let go, you're hurting me, I shouted as if we were in some awful afternoon soap. I suppose it was part of the game, might as well be clear about that. However, as I still didn't know whether I wanted to say yes or no, I suppose I can't complain. I bawled at Him a second time but He thrust his huge paunch against me, wedged between us. He squeezed my cheeks with one hand until I opened my mouth while with the other He pushed my back, forcing me forward on to my knees. I know, know only too well that was the moment the expression on my face changed, looked strange, and my eyes became scary, bottomless pools. I don't know if it is an expression of defiance or a war cry. It certainly isn't the gaze of a victim or fugitive. It's quite mysterious, but my pupils go dark and the way I gaze at the person opposite me changes imperceptibly around my eyes, when all that starts to happen, I think they can see into my soul. Maybe you think it's hard to describe yourself like that but I can tell you it's how I see myself reflected in the way my lovers see me. When I wiped your windows, however, I was also thinking

about the finger marks I'd left on the white wall in my house, and
about the door that was still ajar.

The writer can't work with all this noise, he will tell her to
come at another time, on a day when he's not there, maybe,
in the evening. No, a cleaning lady can't come in the evening,
or at the weekend or on holidays... Besides... She seems like
a woman with other things to do, she's not an elderly lady
wearing rope sandals and a plaid housecoat. If anyone these
days still wears plaid housecoats. He repeats that compulsive
gesture of clicking on the icon of his e-mail (none), the other
address (junk mail), returns to the front page of a foreign daily,
a national daily and finally opens up his word document with
the cursor on the blink. Nobody can work like this. All that
time he could hear her movements as she cleaned the windows
that look over the street, her deep breathing reminds him how
poor his concentration is. He had to endure her whole routine,
and she seems to have ignored him from the time she came in.
She knows he is there and that he's quite close but she's only
said hello. A peculiar person, that's for sure. Two strangers
in a house who can only manage one 'hello'. It's his fault, the
writer thinks, he's the one in charge, who takes the decisions,
and that's maybe why she's only addressed him with that
initial hello. What if he intrudes? What if she doesn't like being
asked about her life? Because he's completely ignorant about
her, and the fact is he can't talk to her about the weather, the
news, or the road works. Isn't it hot? No, that's too predictable.
Be that as it may, she will soon know all there is to know about
him: by tidying his drawers, touching his things, changing his

sheets, going into his bathroom and seeing what products he does and does not use. She'll soon know everything about the writer and he still can't decide how to categorize her, where to slot her. He only knows her name.

I've never told you but I was really intrigued those first few weeks I cleaned your house. I've told you how peaceful and quiet the atmosphere was, but I was really fascinated by you, sir. You weren't like other men, not like the ones I was used to meeting. When you looked at me, you did so in a way I couldn't understand. It wasn't transparent like the gaze of lovers that search and try to find out your secrets. You looked at me as if you wanted to get to know me and at the same time as if you felt kindly towards me. And that all happened before you knew me at all, before I'd told you a thing. To be sure, who'd have thought we'd end up talking so much. And now I look back with the distance my new life affords, and I think how lucky I was to meet you. Why were you so well disposed to me then? I was annoyed by the way you scrutinized me as if I wasn't there. And even more annoyed when I felt you knew more about me than I did myself. At the time it riled me when I didn't find the slightest flicker of desire in your eyes. I don't know if I ever tried to provoke you, if only to stop feeling irritated that you were so close but never tried it on.

Would you like a coffee? He's already brought you a cup, American style, without even asking if you wanted milk or sugar. He's made it like his, with skimmed milk and two lumps. She turns round upset as if she'd forgotten he was there, all that time she'd been thinking how peculiar for two strangers to be in a house and not say a word to each other. Momentarily he felt sour and disappointed, as if the importance of her presence for him wasn't on a level with his importance for her. The young woman hangs her cotton duster on the ribbon around her waist and takes the cup. She steadies it with both hands in a gesture that makes her seem like a child, even more so when she blows and looks up to say thank you. She might have seemed shy with that gaze that appeared to come from nowhere and broadened out instead of simply deferring. Young girls look up, then down, but she reacts in line with her previous bodily reaction when taking the steaming cup. She smiles faintly. I'm very sorry I could only do the kitchen and the bathroom the other day. It was just that everything was so dirty... I mean... Don't worry, you do as you think best. And the writer stares at her. Is everything all right? It's a straightforward enough question, but when he looks at her like that there must be a hidden agenda. Yes, I'm fine, just very tired. That's right, you work nights, don't you? Almost always. She looks him straight in the eye again, very briefly. If only one could describe precisely the thousands of ways of gazing, the intent behind such a common, everyday movement with all the shades of meaning that language allows. This is where the writer glimpses the limitations of his trade: there are places words can't take you. He would invent a code made from glances, record and play them back time after time to work out all their hidden meanings. The code would be so important he'd have to be careful it didn't fall into dangerous hands, a tool with unimaginable power, the power to strip souls bare. But he had a long way to go; it would require lots of dedication and effort. He saw that the moment the idea occurred to him and realised he hadn't even read her eyes that were still waiting for the script to develop. What can you see now? she seems to be asking as she sips unenthusiastically. I don't know, do you? But he simply looks at her looking down into her cup and blowing on her coffee.

I now know exactly what you mean when you ask how I am or how things are. I didn't then. The phrases you used are usually quite empty, people ask how you are and don't even wait for your reply. On the other hand, when you asked me I always felt I had to reply truthfully. The first day you took me completely by surprise, I suddenly felt uneasy simply because of the way you waited to hear my reply. It was from that point on that I had no choice but to start thinking about the state I was in. As I did so, to avoid the unease caused by the fact it was the first time I'd done that and was at a loss, I stirred my spoon slowly, looked into my cup, then anywhere, a quick glance at the floor or the doors still carrying marks from my cleaning cloths. I thought you were thinking I acted like that out of shyness when it was simply my way of ruminating. Well, to begin with it was perhaps a way of avoiding having to tell you the truth. Especially because when my eyes met yours again you were still there, patiently awaiting my reply, whatever that might be.

Long hours? From ten to six. Where? Do you know the cold sausage and pizza factory on the outskirts of the city? Well, there. I work in the pizza room. Almost always. And don't you find it hard to sleep by day?

Do you remember how long it took me to reply? You took pity on me, but not in any scornful way. I see that now.

It's not, if people don't wake you up. I lower the shutters, have very thick curtains and wear earplugs. I often don't bother about them: when I wear them I get more rest, but I sometimes think my ears can't breathe. If nobody bothers me, I can sleep straight through; as I bed down at seven, when there's not so much light or noise… The worst is when someone rings the bell. They often ring the wrong one, or it's that young lad who brings the business post or the postman or the men who come to read the gas meters. I get up and drag my feet and shout what? as loud as I can. They must think I'm a lazy so-and-so, a person who sleeps in very late, and they answer in a tone that sounds incredibly shrill. They don't know what it's like… trying to get back to sleep after you've seen it's a lovely day and the light slips into your flat through some crack because I've not lowered the shutter completely. But sometimes it's friends who've forgotten I work nights.

Haven't you ever thought of doing some other kind of work? You are young, after all. Yes, I know, everybody asks me that, and what can I say? I like cleaning. Obviously, I could have done other things, I passed all my exams at secondary school, you know? But when it was time to choose a profession, I found it so difficult to decide that I chose to look for a job while I thought it over. And you soon get used to having money of your own. Or maybe I've never really thought through what I wanted to be when I grew up. I'm now beginning to think that cleaning may be a job for life. You know what happens when I am cleaning? I can really forget myself and everything I do has an immediate outcome, I know what the results of my work are. I tell you this because nobody believes me when I say I like cleaning, but I've tried other things and not liked them so much. What I do know is that I won't go back to studying.

the first stranger

She looks perfectly posed seen from the angle of the doorway: on her feet, legs slightly flexed, elbows on thighs, digging into them non-stop. She's streaming in sweat yet again, sweat that marks out her temples and glues down the first line of her hair. Her nostrils swell and fold at a steady rhythm, and glow. Every movement seems to firm up her cheeks, and moist lids are all you can see of her eyes, the corners of which dribble trickles of soot. When she stoops over she reveals the top of her breasts that rise and fall in step with her breathing. She's concentrating, now and then wipes away the splashes that hit her face, apparently unsurprised and certainly not upset by them. She grips the white surface, quickens her actions, then stands up straight, looking pleased.

I can tell you I had my doubts on my first visits here. I was keen to find out about you, that's for sure. When I saw your pyjamas on a pillow at the foot of your bed, your bed not properly made ... It bothered me to see your comb in the lavatory in the lobby, an ancient-looking comb. I could see you were all smart with your hair parted and didn't know if you'd just combed it before I arrived. I tried to clean your things quickly, as if I wasn't

collecting information about you from every nook and cranny,
but at the same time I registered every detail with a curiosity
that intrigued me to the tips of my fingers, the curiosity of
caresses that escape of their own free will.

The writer who's been stressing for some time about the
private terrain she has invaded just has to go as far as his
bathroom and watch her from afar, from the passage. He can't
decide whether he regrets or not the fact she's been cleaning
his toilet bowl. It certainly makes him feel uneasy. It's her
job, he tells himself, while he watches her give the bathroom
a quick sweep with the small broom. Surely he must have
left something there, before she went in, some evidence of
his private life? What could be more private than that? He'd
thought of cleaning the space himself, but immediately thought
better of it: what if she was upset he didn't trust her enough?
He'd also thought of cleaning it and not saying anything, but
cleaning the same place twice would have been a waste of
resources. Besides, she'd have noticed. That would have meant
her cleaning what's clean, what's spick and span. Interfer-
ence in her professional work, after all. As if his publisher had
written his novels to save him the bother. But the writer likes
writing and she... she says she likes cleaning, but perhaps
she doesn't really. Or perhaps she does, apparently there are
women who experience a kind of pleasure doing the things the
rest of the world detests. Men too, but mainly women. Right
now, for example, she seems task-driven, seems really intent
on what she is doing... right, as if she were having sex, and even
more so when splashes of water from the bowl occasionally hit

her face and she seems to be enjoying that. He should have asked her: do you like washing toilets? But he soon sees that is hardly a respectful question and is more useful from the perspective of his curiosity as a novelist than for x-raying her present state of mind. When you observe them, people turn into objects, but the writer knows that even when they are fictitious they slip through your fingers and make their own way in life. She is flesh and blood. So much flesh and blood she has suddenly realized that he was there and has put down the cloth she was using to wipe the toilet lid.

Before I guessed you were behind me I was re-playing, like a film, the first time I got involved with a stranger, a few weeks after starting to work in the factory. He sat at the back of the dining room, alone, by the coffee machines that make noise throughout the night, and sank a fork into his snack box. He was stooping but maybe that was the uncertainty the first time you work nights causes. People struggle to get used to it, and become gloomy when they think they're not at home when everyone else is. Not seeing that dodgy night-time programme, not falling asleep on the sofa, not waking up startled by the louder volume of an advertisement and realizing they'd dozed off when they see the spittle staining the cushion. They also miss going to bed naturally, lying down and switching the light off when it's still dark. This is the bottom line, the main difference between those who work nights and those who work days: that when they go to bed, it isn't dark. The dark of night means you are inside something and being inside a huge hangar is like being nowhere at all.

That's why I always felt sorry for the new workers. Maybe

because I remembered how I'd started out and a lump formed in my throat or stomach or wherever and I'd keep breathing deeply so as not to feel bloated. I'd swell under my lungs and walk like a hunchback. Exactly the same posture as that stranger whose name I soon got to know, although don't imagine that meant he was no longer a stranger.

I didn't see that then, but I always acted the same way towards newcomers. I looked them out and sat with them during food breaks. I usually preferred to go to the changing rooms outside the hangar, the one belonging to their company, where nobody looks at you. It didn't feel comfortable sitting in their dining room with coffee machines and workers in white or pale green who came in and ate a pizza fresh from the oven, knowing that we couldn't do that unless we asked for special permission, simply because we wore blue. That's why I also ate in the outside locker rooms, even though it was cold and they were small. I didn't want pale greens and whites walking by and staring at me, probably checking on the time I spent there.

But I made an exception that day when I saw the newcomer, who was sitting close to the coffee machines, and I said hello, can I sit down? Of course, he said yes and that's how we ceased to be strangers in name.

The guy looked shy, so I looked at him in a friendly way to cheer him up. But I soon realized he was looking at me quite differently. His eyes started to go watery and very dark. I immediately knew what he was after. Especially when I'd talked to him about the time he'd been with the firm and if he'd done nights before or not and he said that he'd done more window-cleaning on tall buildings than industrial cleaning; he took advantage of the fact the pressure from my diaphragm meant he was lower down than me to peep at my body under the blue overall, because I'd not zipped up completely. One side had folded over to make an inside lapel. I then realized he'd guessed I wasn't wearing any clothes underneath, and my skin was taut from the heat. I put my hand on my zip and said, Oh! It's so hot in the fermenting rooms! I've been in there more than two hours removing dough balls from under the production line and the smell of the yeast has stuck to my hands, smell this, and he grabbed my wrist and sniffed.

The lavatories on the top floor were the least used. But they were just as dirty and as the noise from the whole factory was drowning out my panting I didn't think the overseers would hear my cries inside those lavatories where the floor was covered in paper and the stainless steel sinks were a dull grey. To tell you the truth, I barely had time to get close to the stranger and smell him, because after he'd said let's go and we'd walked into the lavatories he was on top of me straightaway. Almost no time passed between him saying that and sticking his fingers inside me. He was hurting me. I tried to get rid of his hand by kissing him, but I soon found I didn't like the taste of him. I didn't have time to try again because he'd gone down on me too far kissing me in another direction. No, he wasn't kissing me, in fact, he was gobbling me with unseemly haste. Then I thought what a cheek, they start eating your cunt up in no time. And what if he wants a little payback after? If I'd not liked the taste of his mouth, what chance was there I'd like the taste of his penis? That's why I told him to stop it, but it was too late because my palms were pressed against the plywood lavatory walls, and my head was lolling against the rough, unplastered surface.

You frightened me, I didn't hear you coming. He tells her he's taking a short break from what he is writing, that he sometimes gets annoyed with himself because he doesn't know how to continue the story. He remarks that she looks as if she's hardly slept.

No, we had a very busy night in the factory and it took me a long time to get to sleep. A very long time. You know what happens? When you work days, if you're feeling stressed out when you get home, you do things, get the dinner ready, maybe, go shopping, get some fresh air, watch telly and when it's time to go to bed, that's all forgotten, but when you work nights it's not like that at all. If I get home just before seven and start doing things to relax myself, it's soon eight or nine, and, obviously, now it's broad daylight, I can't trick myself into thinking I sleep at night, that I went to bed last night like everyone else, and that's why I hardly got any sleep today. It's a question of awareness, if you are aware it's daytime you can't deceive yourself by saying it's night. And wouldn't you like to change to days? I don't know, I've been doing this for a long time now and I'm used to it. Maybe I would, maybe it would do me good to start sleeping at night again, but I would lose the night shift bonus. And doesn't it make family life and every-thing else difficult? No, not really, I don't do family life very much anyway, I find it's a drag. And the friends I have now are from the night shift. Maybe that's why I gradually lost my friends from secondary school, because when I'm awake they are asleep and when I'm asleep they are at work. It might even be an age thing. And what do you do to meet new people? She puts the lavatory lid down and sits on it, twirling a wet cloth. Well, you know, as nobody wants to do that kind of work, there's a big turnover in our team. New people keep coming all the time. There are also the factory workers, but we have next to nothing to do with them, they always look down on us as if we came from another planet and they were superior beings.

skin on the carpet

She is lying on the cold floor flat on her back with her splayed, folded legs sheathed in threadbare jeans. Her arm movements bare part of her belly, but only now and again. From here you might think she's been beheaded, or was a body on a cold surface made from perfect squares stuck together by white putty. Might just, if you couldn't see the taut underside of her chin and the thin skin drawn tight over her gullet, which rises and falls even though she's on a hard floor gleaming with the light sweat from her back. But a bit further down, at the bottom tip of the triangular opening of her faded T-shirt, you can see a pool of liquid. And all because she's on a very flat surface and her breasts make a hollow when she raises her arms, a movement that covers the dip with a glossy patina that reflects everything around. Her sweat reflects objects, the light and the gaze of the writer, who stands there observing her still on her back with her legs splayed and folded.

When I cleaned under all his cupboards I couldn't stop myself from feeling I was entering swampy territory from which I might never emerge. Whenever I was cleaning his house my thoughts went at a different rhythm. My memories settled like fake snow in a glass globe. Right, this is how I see it so easily now with hindsight. Though it was extraordinary the way I could now bring order into the images from my topsy-turvy life. When I was under that cupboard, for example, I could see myself the previous day, moving up and down, frantically, trying to make rapid progress, trying not to think how the carpet in the dining room in my new house was wrinkled and rough and I kept scraping my knees with every movement I made. I tried not to think how it would hurt later because, you know, my skin sometimes takes time to communicate the feeling of pain to my brain. That's why whenever I pressed my pelvis against his pelvis I didn't feel a minute layer of skin sticking to the material, scraps that neither I nor other specialists in minute scraps of dirt would ever find among the knotted fibres. He never stopped talking, mouthing one sentence after another, never listening to himself. I never did dare tell Him that perfect sex is completely silent, only the panting, moans and fast breathing give it the genuine sound for what it is, an elemental act with no rational baggage, yielding to an energy that is different to whatever leads you to do other things, different to cleaning. Shut up! I should have told Him to shut up so I could hear my own murmuring and feel his orgasm that came after mine. I let my head loll backwards and He simply looked at my nostrils that flared open and closed, my half-open mouth, and the way I bite my lip. It was then that I desperately wanted Him not to say a single word. And just look at me. Then I could have heard myself, both of us in tandem, and not his chatter interrupting my thoughts. If only He'd been even slightly original, but he spoke as if He'd stolen every sentence from a porn film. I'm not being vain, but the thought that I could only drag the most predictable words out of Him made me feel cheap and nasty. As if any other woman could have played my part and He'd have said yes, yes, yes, like that, like that, go on, don't stop, and so on. In a flash I bent over and gripped his body tight while one hand brusquely sought out his lips and He took it in his mouth. That shut Him up.

He only shut up like that or with his own orgasm. It was worse when our bodies separated and He chattered on as if He'd never shut up. He said He'd brought lunch with me in mind, how perhaps I wouldn't want to go out and would need to sleep some more. I stared at Him willing him to clear off, why didn't He go once and for all? I was sleepy, not really hungry, and I told Him I was going back to bed. He had half taken the plastic containers out of his bag, then put them on the side of the kitchen and came to get me. No, no, no, have lunch with me, I don't want lunch by myself, then I could stay on and have a siesta. But I already had one cheek on a pillow, my arms spread either side of my body, and my back felt completely relaxed. He caressed the middle of my back and my one exposed ear. Why don't we invent some new caresses? I love discovering new caresses with you. I was half asleep and told Him there were no new ones to invent. Come on . . . Isabel. I fell asleep as I felt Him pecking along my arms, and when his pecks reached my cheek I could smell his heavy, thick breath, that was disgusting, not soothing.

What's the matter, have you lost something? he asks, even though he can see her arms cleaning under the cupboard, and has been watching her work for some time like that. What did you say? Have you lost something, the writer repeats, starting to get anxious for some reason or other. No, you have to clean *under* the cupboards as well. People don't realize this, they imagine you only need to wipe the dust off furniture but the space underneath is important too. I've been thinking about this cupboard of yours for days, and I couldn't leave it today. I wouldn't be able to sleep thinking about the mounds of dust lurking there or, worse still, the cobwebs. Can you see? And she shows him a dark black duster and looks pleased with herself. She grips the cupboard with both hands and pushes so her whole body slid over the ground and then pushes herself up with the fingers of both hands. She goes phew and hangs the duster back on her belt. Have *you* finished your work, sir? No, I mean, my work is never finished, I've always more to do. That's the lot of us writers too, we're always working though it seems we never are. I sometimes work, even when I am asleep. Well, how awful, I don't envy you that. When we've clocked out of the factory, we've clocked out, not a minute more to the company. The writer looks at her rather than listens, that's what his work is, scrutinizing what people are like, seeing inside them unawares and trying to connect what they say and what they really mean. He hides behind words. He looks deep into her eyes, at her hands that speak for themselves, at the curve of her spine, the way she looks at him while he talks about work and for a moment it seems she is watching him watching her, trying to see deep inside. She might be afraid he was X-raying her like he does the individuals who then turn into his characters, especially now he has madly fled his computer and the cursor that click-clicks silently. Don't you ever get tired of writing? She watches him run a hand through his hair, like a comb, and he looks away from her, to one side, at the wall behind her. Or looks nowhere and only looks away from her in order to think. Because if he thinks while he's staring at her she might get upset. No, it's something I like doing. It's my trade, after all. But you're shut up here all day by yourself. No need to suffer on my behalf, I'm not as alone as you think. The writer smiles, wanting to draw her in, but she hasn't heard him, and is knocking a wisp of hair from her face and she says yes, she understands, he's got his characters for company.

I would never say this to your face, but I think it's true: a few weeks after I'd been coming to your house I realized that you needed that time as much as I did. Well, maybe I'm exaggerating slightly, maybe I didn't realize so soon and only grasped that much later on, but it is true: you needed me as much as I needed you. Only in very different ways.

The writer knows what's happening because he has been a professional for some time and knows his own processes perfectly. But he is sometimes overcome by his harpy syndrome and he and the harpy keep themselves company for a few days, sometimes months. If he hadn't published lots of books that many people have read, he might think his whole life as a writer had been a long journey in the company of the harpy who tells him that what he does is trivial, unimportant and that he is only deceiving himself if he believes he's going to make it with that shit.

That's why he is talking to her now. He stops staring at her and takes advantage of a pause to ask her if she lives alone. All alone, that's why I need to work overtime. I work at the factory on Saturdays if there's work, because it's well paid. And don't think that my house is that big, but I live all by myself... The writer starts to enter that area of gossip writers so adore and is dying to know if she has a partner, though tentatively, it's too soon to test those waters and asks her instead, don't you have any children? No, first I have to find someone I want to have them with, don't you reckon? She says no, changes her posture, puts her weight on her other leg, hand on waist, still holding the duster that dangles down. Oh, well, you're young, you'll soon find someone. I'm not what you'd say completely alone, I have like a... how do they say? A relationship, but nothing very serious. You know how difficult things are today when it comes to men. Don't you think they are very difficult? Well, I don't know, I'm not looking for a man. Well, I'll tell you a few stories that will show you there are no real men anymore, I don't know where they hide out. And the women I work with would tell you as much. They've all had children with different fathers or boyfriends who beat them or are a waste of time. They often say that good men don't exist, and I'm beginning to believe them. Don't feel offended, I don't really know you yet. No, don't worry, if they say that's the case, they must be right in part. You know, there's not much to choose between jerks and queers these days. Her eyes linger on a ray of light illuminating one of the squares on the floor and watch a solitary ant walk across it. The writer turns and scrutinizes her once again and she feels trapped, forced to follow the thread of what she's just said. I'm not to blame, you know? To blame for what?

To blame for the fact there aren't any good men anymore. She doesn't understand why he doesn't say he doesn't agree, why he doesn't react and leave if he feels offended, why he doesn't stop gazing at her, trying to find out what could have happened for her to say such a thing to him only a few weeks after they've met. She would expect the writer to say no, that he is different, but he simply gazes at her. I never said you were to blame. And then he smiles.

I always liked your smile. And the bad jokes you kept repeating. But right at the beginning, until not very long ago, I felt terribly embarrassed about liking your smile and the way you suddenly went all serious before making an observation that would catch me quite on the hop. Now I'm beginning to understand why I was so embarrassed, but I didn't at the time. In fact, I was embarrassed at being embarrassed because I found you so relaxing and because I felt so at ease when I was with you. I was upset to think that one day you might find out.

Saturday

By now the writer was used to her weekly presence. He'd miss her if she didn't come, although that might seem a slight exaggeration. *Didn't I say we needed each other, that it was mutual? Yes, you could have quietly got on with your life if I had suddenly stopped cleaning your flat, but I doubt I'd ever have saved myself from myself if I hadn't continued my visits. In any case, for some strange reason a terrible fear gripped me when I was near your house and I bawled to high heaven inside my head I don't want to go.* The writer tolerates her silences and clatter in the kitchen, her heavy breathing that is now part of his everyday life. Today she arrives late all hot and bothered and says I'm sorry I'm so late and hangs up her bag and coat and gathers up her hair, gripping a clip between her teeth and says she overslept. The writer says fine, not to worry, but she's already in the gallery looking for her tools, he can hear her and finds her reassuring.

She runs a micro-fibre cloth over the kitchen doors that seems to leave circles but disappear straight away. Because micro-fibre is the best thing going and she knows exactly how quickly she needs to wipe the cloth, the secret is not to dally too long. The writer leaves her a cup of steaming coffee on the side and she says thank you. I really am very sorry, it won't happen again, I promise. Don't worry, you were only ten minutes late. I know, but I don't like to be silly over work, these things are sacred and I don't want to be late again, it's not me. That's a promise. What do you mean by it's not me? I'm never late. I never oversleep. That's sacred. But I've been sleeping very badly the last few days. I've not been sleeping at all, in fact. Well, perhaps there's no need to be so severe with yourself. In this case, I should be. And are you as severe with everyone? She turns round holding the cloth she'd like to wring out between her fingers and sees he's analyzing her once again. You're very clever, aren't you? You like playing at being a psychologist? Well, no, I'm not like that with other people, but I am different. What do you mean by different? Are you so perfect you never arrive late? Do you never make mistakes? You know… forgive me for saying this, but you are pissing way off target. Just think for a moment how I've only got myself, if I fuck up, I fuck up and there's nobody to come to my rescue. Can you understand now?

And you, sir, have you finished that book? He shakes his head but she'd already anticipated what his reply would be because she always asks the same question. She just can't fathom how he spends the whole day shut up at home and never finishes anything. Some day I'd like you to choose one of my books, he told her one day, and I'll give it you as a present, but she said no thanks very much. What I do like are travel guides, if you ever have one you don't need, whatever the country, don't think twice about giving it to me, I'd be delighted. The writer tiptoes around his disappointment, thinking how stupid you are trying to get a cleaning lady to read. So what's your book about then, if I might ask? Don't worry I'm not going to read it, but I can see it's taking you so long. Is it? But you've only been coming for a couple of months! I've been writing this book for the past two years. Hell, that sounds like hard work. How long have you been cleaning at the factory? Please, there's no comparison. I repeat the same actions time after time. There are six, no seven pizza production lines, and they've just installed a new one to make mini-pizzas, but I always repeat the same operation. Hose down the lot to get rid of the worst and sluice the bits of food down the drain, soap up all the machines and then hose them down. That's the bit I like most. You can't imagine what it feels like to hold the hose when the water is jetting out so power-fully from the big nozzle and seems to have a life of its own. And it's us cleaning women who hold it in both hands and direct that energy at the most out-of-the-way corners of the cheese and ham dispensers or the conveyor belts that never stop running. I like to do the high machines, raising my arms to lift the hose up or even better when I have to climb to the top of a ladder. It makes you ache all over, but it's a good way to make you feel you're really alive. I expect you think I'm half crazy, don't you?

Are you OK like that? She's now kneeling on the kitchen side cleaning the top of the cupboards and suddenly turns round and looks at the writer in a way that disconcerts him, says I'm OK and shrugs her shoulders. You, sir, still haven't told me what's in your book, you didn't give me an answer. She stretches her arm until she can reach over the cupboard tops and runs the cloth there though she can't see up there. It's the story of a cleaning lady. She looks at him and smiles, hey, come on, not even you can believe that. And why not? Because, sir, that's of no interest to anyone. If no one wants to clean how do you expect anyone to be interested in reading about what a cleaning lady does? Every life is interesting. You cleaning ladies have your secrets too, don't you? She continues making circling movements with her arms and talking, actions that make her stop in mid-sentence. Well, I don't know about secrets, but there is *life* in the factory, though it's the sort that makes you want to weep. I'm writing the story of a woman and her relationships with men. She stops dead and stares at him. And do you know enough about women to invent that kind of thing? No, I know about men. She stares at him incredulously and thinks it odd his eyes never blink when she stares him out. She gets agitated when he doesn't as if she were an object that someone is scrutinizing in a shop window. So maybe you can help me. Maybe I can, she replies intriguingly. You mean because of your steady boyfriend? She's now started moving again and lets the writer continue to observe her while she works and talks.

I don't have a steady, I told you, He's a bastard and is not my boyfriend. She jumps down with a dull thud and sips her coffee as if she is afraid someone else might run off with it. You know, there's something about your house? It's a nice place to be, you feel protected against the outside world. It's a bit like a safe haven, isn't it? I'm glad you feel you like that here, but what's wrong with your boyfriend? What does he do to you? Oh, nothing really, He bothers me all the time. He bothers me when I am asleep and you can't imagine how annoying it is to be bothered when you sleep during the day. And you know, He couldn't care less, couldn't care less if I rest or not. You know what men are like. Just saying this brings a flush to her cheeks and she says, well... I mean... There are no men anymore, you know, it's not like it used to be when there were real men around, now I don't know what's the matter with them, they're either gay or worse. Worse for us, I mean, for us women. It's hopeless. And He takes advantage of the fact there are no real men anymore. They either go looking for them abroad, so they do everything for them like their mothers, or they're perverts. The writer smiles faintly and says nothing until she starts talking again. It must be quite a problem if He works during the day, right? No, it isn't. He can come and go in his work as He pleases. Not like you, sir, at home all the time, but He can leave his office and say He has a visit, He doesn't need to make excuses. But I'm fed up with Him waking me up when I am asleep and I sometimes think I'd prefer to be by myself, all nice and quiet. Don't you reckon? I suppose so, they do say 'better alone than in bad company'. The writer opens his mouth to continue what he's saying, but, her eyes glazing over for a moment as if lost in her own thoughts, she suddenly interrupts him animatedly.

You know what the problem is? He's very annoying and He ought not to be. If I'd wanted someone to make life difficult and annoy me I'd have looked for somebody to live happily together with, as they say, but I don't want hassles and that's why I have Him, a lover. But lovers who stay around aren't lovers any longer, they become something else we don't have a name for. You, sir, know so much about words, maybe you know what a person like that is called. I'd say He was a steady boyfriend. No, I told you He can't be, no way.

He dropped by a lot those days. He came around a lot more and maybe after that conversation with you I wanted to find out what there really was between us. I started to want to see Him again to find out if I was beginning to like Him too much, if what I liked was the fact He liked me, or was it just that I wanted to feel the weight of his body on mine. You see, it was your fault if all of a sudden I shoed myself into the role of the typical lover. I was sitting on the sofa looking at the blank television and holding my mobile. I knew it wasn't the day or the time to do it, but I wrote Him a text: want to come over? I was one step away from pressing send, I'd selected the contact number but was hesitating, thinking about two possible replies: 1, that He'd say yes, but that was unlikely, 2, that He'd say no and the state that would reduce me to, thinking how stupid you are to think you are in a relationship, I should have whipped myself mentally, cried can't you see that He's the one who always decides? There remained a third possibility I'd not considered: that He was totally noncommittal, neither yes nor no, making it clear that wasn't the right day because it wasn't our usual day or time and He had another life to live. I put both feet on the table while I thought about the fallout that would bring while I looked at the small screen. 1 or 2 or, even worse, the option I'd not considered. If it had been 1, that could never have been the case, it would have meant his relationship is more than the occasional bodily encounter. Will He ask for something more besides? Would I be prepared for such an unexpected outcome? I took my feet off the table that I wiped with the palm of my hand. I took a deep breath to re-energize myself and pressed send, holding my mobile at arm's length and closing my eyes as if it was about to explode in my hands. When I saw 'message sent' blood rushed to my head and I thought I was going to be sick, my eyes suddenly clouded over and my heartbeat quickened.

Then there was that terrible wait after I put the device down on the coffee table and decided to forget all about it, act as if it didn't exist and stretch out on the sofa and put one arm over my eyes. I kept sniffing my arm in a futile attempt to find a trace of Him. I explored every centimetre of skin but found none. I told myself I was fine, but kept tapping the back of the sofa, stretched my legs, tucked them into the foetal position until I made an effort, pulled myself up and went straight to the lavatory. I looked at myself in the mirror, particularly my eyes and the area around them, I didn't have rings, that day. I pressed my bottom eyelid down like a doctor, but couldn't diagnose a thing. Whether I was healthy or ill. Whenever I looked into a mirror, I always went through the same routine. Fucking bastard, I thought, He won't answer, you just see. Humiliation. Pride makes you think like that. He's not so keen on you, or He would reply at once. But He'll be busy with something or other, or his mobile is switched off, or she's next to Him or He's playing with his daughter or taking the dog for a walk or the rubbish out or is watching a film, or is at the cinema or the theatre or they're both cycling happily away with the little chair behind. I thought I might like to have a photo of her so I could put a face to her when I was imagining her, whether she was fat or thin, dark or light-skinned, pretty or plain. Stress made me smooth out the skin under my eyes until I looked grotesque, a caricature in the mirror. Ugly.

I could still hear the message alert that had buzzed on the sofa. Text messages take so long to open, that one was taking so long! Can't today, you know, it's Saturday. I'm sorry. The fucking bastard! Though obviously, I didn't say that to Him. He wasn't thinking about me, not even just up for a fuck. I returned to the mirror but came back straightaway. With my thumb I wrote Don't worry, OK, I'll get someone else.

And I did. I texted one of those strangers in the factory and asked him if he wanted to meet up. He took his time to reply and when he did I'd gone to sleep with the lights switched on. Where do you live, asked the stranger.

But you do like him, don't you? You know, I couldn't really say … I suppose I do or I wouldn't let Him in, but He has things I like and things I don't, like anyone. The writer stares at her and, for a moment, she feels like he's looked inside her, somewhere unknown to herself. What? No, I didn't say anything. Are you sure you don't want me to tidy that pile of clothes? No, don't worry about that, I'll do it when I have a moment. She climbs back up and he walks back along the passage and is reunited with his cursor.

razor blades

She's cleaning more energetically than ever today. Moves frantically from one end of the flat to the other and seems not to be following her usual routine. She does the kitchen, first the cupboards, the burners on the oven top, the fridge, then swept up with the broom. She always did the lavatories, dusted everywhere, the windows too, hung out the carpets to air and finally washed the floor throughout the house. But today she comes and goes, sits on the toilet bowl, gasps and suddenly stops enraptured halfway through cleaning the windows. Until the writer emerges from his office to ask if everything is OK. Everything OK? What he always says when he comes out of his office, so as not to walk past her without breaking the silence. What else could he talk to her about? The weather? The latest political news? His novel? She looks into his eyes and says yes but avoids his gaze. Yes, of course, I'm just a bit tired.

What was I ashamed of that day when I said nothing was wrong? Perhaps because I'd lied. Not to you, but to myself. And just how did you fix it so I couldn't escape my own train of thoughts? It wasn't that I attributed you with special powers, but when you, sir, asked me a question, however ordinary it might seem, your words went in one ear and became the centre of everything. As if your sentences were like the lavatory brush we spin round to remove the shit stuck to the sides of the lavatory bowl. I'm sorry if that seems insulting, it's really meant to be high praise. The last time He'd come was when I was really rested and had slept the whole night. I'd got into bed the moment I arrived home, not before sunrise, though black clouds made it feel like night-time. It was as if it had rained but I'd heard nothing at all. It had been a long time since I'd gone to sleep straightaway without anyone bothering me... My rested body brought me back to life. I got up feeling cheerful. I could feel my back muscles as if they'd stretched all at once and I could pick them out singly in my head. Muscles I'd forgotten about for so long, whose where-abouts I could now define without touching them, the small, sinewy ones under my shoulder blades, those at the back of my waist that spanned my vertebrae. I felt them inside me as if it was an anatomy lesson. You know, I am rarely aware of every part of my body. It was only when I enjoyed that kind of truce that I felt it was mine again. Even the little muscles that weave around the spine, the ones that most often fossilize into hard stones that are difficult to move. It's strange, but when my muscles turn to stone, they don't hurt even more, I suddenly stop feeling them.

But that day was different, I can tell you. When I got up and stretched my back and my arms I felt I was there, whole, and though you will think it odd, that made me feel less alone. As if I had quarrelled with someone I loved deeply and suddenly signed a truce. That's why when I got into the shower, the water wasn't quite as hot as on other days when I would turn the tap until my skin turned red. Not that day when I kept the water at *a pleasant temperature. I felt so good under the spouting water that I decided to make an exception and put in the bath plug. I kept repeating my body, my body, to myself. Still dripping, I rushed off to the kitchen in my bathrobe and boiled up some early evening coffee, with the water making that clean sound. I waited in the kitchen for the coffee to bubble up, hugging my waist. With the reflex reaction of a real professional, I couldn't stop myself running my fingers over the clean kitchen top, along one of the gleaming blue doors where there wasn't a spot of dirt. Doors that were difficult to clean, to begin with the cloth always left a mark, the kitchen was too new.*

When I was just about to get in the water He sent me a message. Can I come and change in your place? I've got an evening meeting. Right, so it is my place, I thought how He'd never used those words before, as if He'd been deliberately avoiding them ever since we met. Come, I texted Him a few moments before plunging in, first my toes, then my whole body, all at once.

When I opened the door He rushed inside in a real hurry, kissed me on the lips, a routine hello kiss and hung up clothes wrapped in plastic in the middle of the passage. Do you mind if I have a quick shower? I've been dashing around all day and I think I need to freshen up. Go on then, I said looking at the expression on his face that wasn't one of desire. He undressed in a flash and left his shoes in the passage. Shoes that had given, that looked grotesque without his feet, a shape that told you what He was like – in his absence. Do you want to put this on? I think you'll like it. He handed me a CD of a man singing in a peculiar accent. Soothing love songs, right? A man who hit the occasional wrong note but seemed to know what love meant. Do singers who talk of love really feel it, or do they put it on to sell records? I liked the first song, the one that goes like this, that says: I don't possess songs, songs possess me. Do you know it? I listened to the whole song on the sofa to the background noise of the water from his shower. He was singing, right? He was singing in my shower and it would be no exaggeration to say He was happy. He was, I mean, He was happy.

Then He put my bathrobe on... Didn't it bother Him putting it on all wet from me? He looked at himself in the mirror as He dried his hair and when He took the towel away it was all standing on end. So funny. I kept glancing at Him from the dining-room door and He looked at me in the mirror and smiled. And what do you expect, I smiled back. I didn't feel like arguing. Then something miserable happened. I leaned back on the doorframe while He spread shaving foam over his face and got his razor blade ready. Whenever He cleaned it under the jet of water He'd look at me as if to say and what now? A what now? that wouldn't wait for an answer. Now I think about it I realize I spend a long time looking at men, as if they were a mystery I was trying to unravel. That hadn't struck me before, but it's the way you have sometimes looked at me, as if you were reading me. Of course, I didn't answer. Not a word. When He'd wiped away the little tracks the razor left between cuts, and the foam near his ears and under his chin, He came over and kissed me on the cheek. Not in a hurry, calmly. He hugged me tenderly, a feeling you don't really recognize until it's so close you can't not feel it, sliding his hands round my waist, then my shoulders, kissing me lightly on the lips, a kiss that seemed to last and last. No slobber, no over-excitement. I don't know if it was because He was so stout but at the time I thought it was the closest I'd ever got to being inside something.

Why don't you stop for a moment? The writer sits in his armchair and crosses his legs. Observation is his work, she thinks. So then, he's observing her. Didn't they let you get to sleep today either? No, I slept but, you know by day... I don't want to spin him the usual, I work nights and do overtime because I want to. I could share a flat and have fewer outgoings or look for a flat that wasn't so new. She tidies her hair behind one ear. Looks this way and that. Forces a smile. Her fingers fiddle endlessly with a loose thread. Sometimes something happens but you don't know what, a pang of conscience, or something, does that ever happen to you, sir? All the time, you always need that feeling of stress to write. I don't write, but now and then *that* hits me and my cleaning is a real disaster. Cleaning should always be orderly, should be consistent from beginning to end, you should never use the vacuum cleaner before you've dusted, or wash the kitchen floor before you've done the cupboards and the fridge. Or... Oh, but none of this is of interest to you. Working nights is OK because you earn more money and with my earnings I can afford to live alone, but working nights turns you into a zombie. No, don't you laugh, can't you see the bags under my eyes? It's not living life, it's living in reverse. When everyone is asleep you are awake and when you work everyone is asleep. You can't ring a friend when you finish work, you can't use a break to... She flexes her arm and squeezes the muscle. But I can't complain,

I have good workmates I can share my problems with – my workmates are a good laugh. They are much older than me and they have experienced so much in their lives they make me feel lucky I'm not like them. You know, men that beat them and such like. They think it's wonderful to find a man who doesn't hit you. She keeps twisting that thread round one finger and another, turning and twisting it with one of her index fingers and looking at it. She opens her mouth as if to say something, lifts the thread up, looks at the writer and is quiet again. She concentrates on the task of twisting it round her finger ever more perfectly. Sir, do *you* not know what men want from women? And forgive me for asking you this question, but the kind of men I know would think me silly if I asked them and my friends would laugh at me and say where've you been all this time? Don't you know that men only have one thing in their head? All the men I've known are like that, though sometimes I wonder if that's the whole truth or a rule without exceptions. I'm no expert, maybe they want to love and be loved in return. She stares up at the sky and smiles shaking her head, it's easy to see that you, sir, spend a lot of time here and don't know what happens in the outside world. The writer shrugs his shoulders. I think I'll die before I see any exceptions to the rule, the one that says, however difficult it may be to stomach, that all men want from women is sex.

cereal moths

She has opened the kitchen cupboard where the writer stores some of his food. She's cleaned these cupboards before, emptied them out and put the packets of rice, dry pasta and tuna on a higher shelf and poured the contents of half empty packets into plastic pots. And there were a lot of half-finished packets. And two or three packets of macaroni. Why start one before you've finished the other? She'd found four or five macaroni at the bottom of a packet that was all screwed up, apparently ready to be thrown away. An almost full one that had already been started and a couple more that were practically empty. And the same with the rice. And the lentils. And different kinds of pasta and flour. What does this guy do with his flour? Bake cakes? Flour for basting, flour for bread, maize flour. Small packets of flan powder and dried fruit. When she opened the cupboard, she could see only heaps and heaps of small crumpled packets and others that were still unopened. That was why she bought all kinds of cheap plastic containers, the kind you put one inside another and gradually emptied all the food into them. She put the macaroni, the different pasta and rice into separate containers. In the end she created a cupboard of countless beautifully arrayed small pots and a heap of crumpled packets on the floor. The process gave her a feeling of great satisfaction, almost of victory. When she'd finished, she looked at everything and sighed proudly.

However, when she opened the doors of a small cupboard today she was frightened by an insect that flew out. A small grey one. No, it isn't grey. What is it? Her eyes follow the insect's flight and watch it settle on the ceiling, on one of the angles it forms with the wall. There seems to be something like a strand of almost invisible cobweb. It's not cobweb, it's much thinner. Not thick enough for a cobweb. The insect stays still while she observes it from as close as she can get, stretching her neck up as far as it will go. She notices how that really thin filament extends into other corners of the kitchen, here and there, intermittently. Especially in the corners. She observes the insect's almost shiny wings. It's not grey, but vaguely brown with a slight sheen. It looks opaque from a distance but close up you can see a shiny coating. Or perhaps it's not simply coating but the whole animal that shines in that indeterminate way. You have to take a long hard look. In fact, it's a golden hue, is, in fact, pretty, but she can only think how it makes her want to puke. A pretty insect? If it's not a butterfly… It doesn't budge, it stays still on the part of the wall where the white is less than white because the air has dirtied it over all these years. She goes back to the cupboard. Where can it have come from if everything was so clean and tidy? She stares at the contents and feels very out of sorts when she is startled to hear the writer's voice by the nape of her neck. He didn't really steal up so close but she was so obsessed by the moths she didn't hear his footsteps and when he spoke it was as if he'd suddenly invaded her space. Do you feel more rested? He's asked her if she was better or just OK. OK, she says and he thinks she's slightly annoyed because he's stopping her from finding out what's really going on in that cupboard. The writer never changes his appearance, always wears the same clothes, and sports the same hairstyle, the same shave. It must be the day of the week when she cleans for him. What can he be like not on that day, not at those times in his flat? What must he be like when he's doing other things apart from just being there? She looks at the skin on his neck. Flabby is what they call it, though that's not the right word. A bit past it, skin that's lived longer than she has and is starting to give up the struggle. Older men are all rather alike. And she is surprised by the way he looks at her, and she blushes brightly.

He had rung in a state when I was looking in the mirror at the brittle lines forming under my eyes. I'd a number that had suddenly appeared. I don't remember when. Perhaps it's all those sleepless nights. I need to see you, to speak to you. Incredulously, I simply replied hey, come on over. You know, when He says I need to see you as if He were in a Venezuelan soap what He really means is I want to fuck you. And I can tell you, by then I was starting to be rather tired of so much passionate sex. When it's passionate every day, I mean, it loses its novelty. I told Him I couldn't, I'd got my period. No, I don't mean that, I really need to see you. Let's go for a drive, go to the mountains, get out of this place.

I went out feeling strange as if I was running away from a kidnapper. Is that so strange? Well, there I was, closing the door trying not to make any noise and watching to see if any of the neighbours saw me leave. And the light of day was so bright I had to shut my eyes, marooned on the pavement clinging to my overcoat. I was convinced He wouldn't come, we'd never gone out together in the street, lunched in any restaurant, we'd never done any of the things couples do when they are getting to know each other. Though, clearly, I wasn't and would never be his partner. And don't imagine for one minute that I wanted to be.

I got into his car but we didn't kiss. He smiled and shook my hand as if it was a work meeting. For a moment I thought I should provoke Him into doing something right in the middle of the street. Grab Him by the neck and kiss Him even if He didn't want me to. Or worse still, look at Him that way while I squeezed his hand so He was forced to resist giving me a kiss because his situation didn't allow him to. If I'd done that I'd have demonstrated what was clearly true but remained unacknowledged by either of us: that despite our repeated encounters it was one huge farce and fake. Why did He suddenly want us to go out like two lovers? I asked what had got into Him and He replied that He wanted to be with me, that it really wasn't so peculiar. Of course it's peculiar, we've never been out of the house together. I feel like doing other things with you, going for walks with you in my favourite places. I must take you to the village where we own a cottage... I'd like to travel with you, what do you reckon? I'll invent some excuse and we'll go to a country you want to visit. One of those you've got guides too. Wherever you want. And what else? What will you say to your wife? Some excuse or other, a congress I've got to go to. I couldn't care less really. I simply want to spend a whole night with you. He went on like that while

I chuckled to myself at how sordid it was – a congress? How predictable, how vulgar from start to finish! He was excited and kept looking from me to the road. What do you reckon then?

I simply soaked up the scenery. To put it mildly, I felt out of sorts when we reached the mountain that smelled so wet and so green.

I won't ask you if you've finished your book. No, you'd better not. It must be very tricky, right? As tricky as life itself, I can't complain.

Do you, as a man, understand what's wrong with men? I find work very easy, but men… are impossible!

Why do you say that?

Because I've known men for a good many years and still can't understand them. I don't know what they want from me, what they are after. They seem to want one thing and then it turns out they want something else. And they all try to con you, to make you think that they only want you to be happy, to have a good time, but that's only a pose. The women in the factory say that all men, without exception, want the same thing from women; even if you get married and have children all men want to do is fuck. I'm sorry! A lot of the women at work quarrel with their husbands, and afterwards you see the men trying to make it up to them when they want a fuck.

So you mean it's not normal for men to be on the look-out for women? Do you really believe they're all the same?

You bet they are! Otherwise you could never explain some of the things they do. They can be so annoying at times! You find them everywhere and always apparently on the point of asking you for something they need from you, that only you can give them. I don't know if you follow me. I'm beginning to get rather fed up with all that, with what men need. I can't understand why they keep coming after me.

You can't understand why you might appeal to a man? Don't you find yourself desirable?

She stares at him and the silence deepens. This guy doesn't even blink, she thinks, he's still staring and she'd have to stop looking at him like that, and does, so she can think about what he's just said. She puts a finger in her ear and wants to scratch hard, keeps turning her nail until she can feel the skin split, oh, that's so comforting. But she's still standing there opposite the writer, who keeps looking at her, waiting for a reply and all she can do is scratch the lobe, very near the ear-hole, though she doesn't stick her nail inside.

Men are different, men like any and every woman. I've never seen a man run any woman down if he thinks he might get a free lay, right? They block out their faces or simply avert their gaze if they are ugly.

The writer says nothing. He simply nods sceptically.

Do you know where these little beggars have come from? I think they're a kind of moth.

a land octopus

She opens the food cupboard again to see if there are any insects left. None. No sign of them. She's defeated them, beaten them, was too much for them. She smiles and is about to shut the doors when one of the jars catches her eye. Just under the pale green lid, an extremely thin thread you can hardly see. She takes the jar and opens it: the lid is covered in traces of moths. How disgusting. She takes a close look, holds it against the daylight coming through the window. How on earth did they get inside? You can't see a single one, they're not flying around, they're nowhere to be seen. Perhaps he knows they are there, the gossamer stuff sticking to the lid sides shows they're still around. But where? She grabs the jar full of rice and shakes it. She steps back alarmed by a flurry of moth wings that fly out frightened by her shaking. They soar past her face en route to the ceiling, all together, skimming her face. But how did they do that? How did they get inside? Then she looks at another jar, shakes its contents, and drives out the insects *en masse*. Then another, and another, and every jar in that small cupboard is full of insects. Every scrap of food is polluted by a sickening film of silk. Blasted insects. Every single jar is in the same state. How awful, how disgusting! She feels her breath quicken. She's horrified.

He came back again when I was asleep. I was in bed between night and day when I guessed the light on my silent mobile was flickering. Real silence would mean it did nothing, didn't warn me in any way that someone was ringing. But that wasn't the case. I closed my eyes, tried to keep warm in my dark bedroom, sheets wrapped round me like a mummy. I could have slept a lifetime, night and day.

He said He wanted to do something special with me... again? We went for a walk in the mountains the other day. I want to sleep right now. Please don't hang up on me, I've got something very important to tell you. Important? I asked snuffling sarcastically. Yes, silly, I'll be with you in a couple of minutes.

His car was full of a voice so squeaky it could have been a man's or a woman's. I've got a fantasy I'd like to make real. Can we swap fantasies? I do what you want and you do what I demand. Ah, so that was the big surprise, although I only thought that, I didn't say as much, I didn't want Him thinking I was expecting anything different, a follow-up to our walk in the woods the other day. Are you sure? I think you might come off worse in that game than me. It must be something we've never done before. I gripped the car door handle as hard as I could and told Him He was crazy and I remembered how He'd gripped my hand, how his fingers were too big for the gaps between mine. I won't do it with another woman looking, if that's what you're after. You men have all got the same perverted fantasies. I don't fancy women. No, it's much simpler than that. Can you see that crag up there, the one with the small church? I really like that place, I often go there when you don't want to see me at lunchtime and survey the whole city from up there. It's not that high up but the view is spectacular. It's a place I've always liked when it's hot and sunny and I can see clearly whether your shutter's up or not or people walking along the streets. Though I also like it when it's foggy or cloudy. You can't see a thing in the fog, but when the clouds are right over you it feels as if they are nearer than they really are, that you can touch them. So near you think you must be shut up in some closed space rather than out in bad weather.

So all this is about setting up a threesome in the church? No, silly, I don't want a threesome. I want to fuck you looking at the city, want to fuck you in my little hideaway. So is that your fantasy? I'm not sure I can handle that. I laughed out loud and looked at Him defiantly, still with the vision of the two of us sitting on the peak, with the mountain against my back, the green at my feet, in my eyes and I was filled with a kind of sadness prompted by something I couldn't pin down. Like all sadness, right? He glanced at me solemnly and said He found the idea very exciting, believe it or not, and that He'd always toyed with the idea but had never found a woman who wanted to do that sort of thing with Him. He said that, opening one side of his mouth, as if saliva was about to trickle out. The obvious question to ask in these circumstances would have been, so what about your wife? Wouldn't she like you to fuck her on the top of a mountain crag looking down over the city? But I gripped myself even harder, sweated and kept quiet…No, obviously, wives don't do that kind of thing. Or at least his didn't. So then, are you up for it? I looked at Him trying to work out what was behind such an odd desire that at the same time was quite banal, what was the catch? But know what? There isn't always a catch. Sometimes we just feel like doing something and that's all there is to it, there's no deep hidden explanation for our desires. What a peculiar fantasy. It's not a threesome, He doesn't want to do it in public (unless there happens to be someone there), or invite another couple, nothing of the sort. For a brief moment I thought I'd won out, thinking, poor wretch, He doesn't realize He could have asked for anything. And if we go and fuck on the mountain, will you do whatever I want afterwards? Yes. Whatever that might be. Yes, whatever you want. What do you want? What would you like me to do that you've never done before? No, that's not fair. I'll do your thing and then I'll tell you. But remember you can't refuse me. OK, OK, I'll let you tie me up and won't complain.

I almost fell down a slope when I stumbled on a stone that rolled right to the bottom among the trees. Yes, you could see the whole city from up there. Even the factory! I heard the stone hit the bottom. He spread out a few chequered napkins over a small flat area. I was really worried under all that earth that was about to fall down! How come mountains aren't dragged down by their own weight? How come they stay upright so easily? He sat down and dusted the thing He'd laid on the ground. The ground was dark. And smelled of countryside, woods and herbs. It really reeked. Reeked as if it were alive. The whole area began to feel peculiar, I couldn't get it out of my head that it was the first time we'd done it not in my place. Silly, I know…He stared at me and I thought his double chin seemed flabbier than ever, his eyes bigger and He was blabbing non-stop. Even when He did stop, his mouth seemed about to open up again. For a moment

I thought his mouth was way too big for his face, that someone must have made a mistake when they assigned those teeth and lips to a face that was far too small. I started to think his eyes were oversize too as He talked and talked, spreading out the cloth and asking me if I wanted to eat before or after. Before or after what, I should have asked. But He didn't give me time to respond because He'd already started on my ear and his trickling saliva was freezing it stiff as usual. I'd just registered that when the excitement started to warm my ear. While He was thrusting away I watched the smoke coming out of a distant factory chimney. A factory where people worked days and slept nights and led normal lives. People who had dinner with someone at night, who ordered a pizza or a Chinese or cooked an omelette and then put their pyjamas on and let sleep gradually take over, like the most normal thing in the world. I so envied the people who worked there. I thought of the very few occasions I'd been able to order a Chinese for dinner and not for breakfast. In fact, none of my meals ever coincided with the rest of humanity's. I had breakfast at noon and had dinner at work. Lunch? I never ate lunch. I could see the pallet truck in the distance and imagined the noise, the stone platters loading and unloading their pizzas when He started exploring my skin, as clumsily as usual, and already heading down to my sex. He really liked doing that and I couldn't find it in me to say that maybe it wasn't what I most felt like doing up there in front of the whole city. In fact, I got quite nervous as He did it, but I gave in and He was like a gummy octopus sucking away inside me, holding on to me with all its tentacles. I let myself go as I imagined that huge octopus had come out of the ground and stuck on me like a sucker. His mouth was like another cunt fucking me, a cunt with tentacles.

I wiped the white flecks from the corners of my lips and cheeks. White flecks that had dried up. I wet my fingers with my saliva and ran them over my skin to remove them. It annoyed me to be left with the taste of Him in my mouth, but it was even more disgusting when it was the taste of me his mouth had put there. I've never liked men doing that kind of thing to me, eating my cunt and then kissing me, I think it's really crude. Maybe some women like a taste of themselves, but I don't. Let alone the smells. Surrounded by all that earth I reckoned it reeked more than in my place. I gulped down some bitter beer that slipped down my throat and hit my stomach with a dull slurp. Breakfasting on beer. He smiled as He finished off the cleaning job on my cheeks. I love you, said He, all of a sudden... After He'd said that there should have been an uneasy silence or a look of surprise on my face, and an I love you too and always want to be with you, leave your wife and come and live with me. It could have been like that, but I spit out a mouthful of beer when I heard Him, and couldn't stop laughing. Hey, stop that, you're pulling my leg. He swung round to look at the city, upset. You're just a whore, how can you laugh now? I was still laughing and telling Him to stop joking around, that even He didn't believe what He'd said. He looked at me indignantly. But aren't we lovers? And aren't you married to a woman with whom you share a daughter? How can you say that you love me? Well, you know, it is what I feel. I don't think you do, you just think you feel like that because you're having a bad time with your wife and you want someone for comfort, but, believe me, love it isn't. You're all mixed up. He said nothing, just looked at the city. Can you just let it drop? I won't say another *word, I can see you feel nothing towards me. What do you mean? Do you want me to tell you that I love you too and that we will be happy together forever and ever? Is that it? We don't start out on an equal footing, so don't you play with me. You have no right to ask anything of me, no right to demand anything. All right, all right, forget it. You and I are lovers, period. Now you tell me what your fantasy is. At that very moment another stone rolled down the side of the mountain.*

She looks at one of the packets of thin pasta that's on a higher shelf and opens it: moths inside there as well. There are some small holes down one side of the packet that are only visible if you look very closely, where someone has folded it in and made a triangle. She opens a packet of really white flour and looks hard and finds a colony of filth-making moths.

She gives everything another once-over with a grimace that could almost be a smile if it weren't one of disgust and splays her fingers in the air. The writer walks into his kitchen. And she can't think how to start telling him what's wrong. What's she done? She didn't do it. It's not her fault. Look, you must throw all this away. The whole lot! You can't use any of this. Look, I don't get how it happened. I left everything clean last week and I thought I'd got rid of all those little beggars, but today. . . I'll go and get some of those strips of paper to hang inside the cupboards and then they'll stick on them. I don't know if they can make you ill, but don't try to salvage any of that food. The writer says no need to worry, you can throw the lot away. She sits on one of the kitchen stools and looks despondent. Well, that's shit. But she doesn't say it angrily, just rather despondently. No need to worry, really. Look, I think I'm too tired to cope, I think I didn't do something right. You do? Why? It happens in the best of households. She keeps her eyes on the floor, so distressed she can't even swallow her saliva.

Mr Impotent

She detects a strange smell in the writer's house. Doesn't *he*? It's an unpleasant smell of rotting, like her cleaning cloths when she doesn't rinse them and they go mouldy and all sticky. That same smell, though stronger, and spreading round the house and up her nostrils. Sir, do you know where this smell is coming from? What smell? replied the writer from inside his study. Do whatever you think's right, I'm on a roll and can't stop now. Can you work with this smell? However, she says nothing and starts sniffing around his rooms, trying to track it down. Not the dining room, the kitchen, the bathroom or the room where he sleeps. From outside in the passage it doesn't seem to come from his study either. In the end, she opens the door into the gallery and the stench gets even stronger. The washing machine! She takes a look and sees it's full. She opens the door and out pours the most horrible stench along with whitish grey water. Greasy water. She gingerly touches the clothes in the washing machine and finds them all covered by a layer of that dubious grease.

That sticky feeling immediately brings up images of her last meeting with Him. He kept me sprawled over the table while

He entered me from behind. Each thrust made the table judder against the wall and I could see it making little holes in the plaster. He sank his fingers into the soft skin between my buttocks and my thighs. He was as on edge as ever, and had to stop now and then because He'd slipped out all unexpectedly. I've told you more than once how clumsy He was. I looked round and He looked at me, I don't know whether compliantly or defiantly. I suddenly felt tired of all that hassle. Why was sex always such a battle? Did it have to be like that? Then it wasn't only the table hitting the wall, it was my flesh that was being impaled on the corner as He gripped me tighter, as sticky as ever. When He finished it seemed as if He was hugging my whole back, as He slumped on top of me and, for a second, I felt his belly pleasantly settle on the small muscles around my backbone.

I turned round to look for the T-shirt I'd thrown on the floor. I didn't look at Him and He didn't look at me and I didn't check inside to see whether I was the same as I was before I came, or to feel the orgasm that normally throbs through me at ever more distant intervals. On that occasion I didn't have to check anything because the only sensation I had was soreness from rubbing my dry skin on his, because He didn't want to wait, was in a hurry. And when I am forced to rush things, I dry up so there's no way it can be a smooth ride. Or maybe I was just tired of seeing so much of him.

He acted as if He wanted to caress me, lifted his hand close to my chin, but I dodged Him and then He started to chatter non-stop, went in and out of the kitchen to see if He could find something for lunch.

This has been going on for far too long. I am tired.

He said He now saw that I didn't love Him, that we only met to fuck, that I'd made it quite clear I wanted only that from Him, and not to worry.

That was obviously a reproach. Can you picture a more typical scene, a man cheating on his wife reproaching his lover for not loving him? Of course it would have been easy enough to let myself be carried away by his fantasy, and for Him to come and live in my place happily ever after. Yes, that's as ridiculous as it sounds. But you know how these happy endings turn out. I had much more at stake than He did. Words of reproach spurted out like so much spit and queued impatiently under my teeth, under my tongue. Words like his life was all sorted, that He was staking nothing. Words like bastard and son of a bitch, and why do you want me to commit myself when you know perfectly well there's no future in it. And for the first time the number one question rolled up my throat and over my tongue like a gob of bile: why didn't He do all that with his wife? Why wasn't He able to solve the problems He had with her, why did He always immediately resort to other women? Didn't He love her after all that time? After having a daughter with her, after spending every night of his life with her? I'd have said all that, but I'd already promised myself I wouldn't interfere in his life. What would He have said anyway? The usual clichés about wanting to find what He couldn't get at home? That things hadn't been going well with her for so long? That they had problems? Whenever I've been with married men I've always thought they should keep their explanations to themselves. For some odd reason, however, they often felt obliged to tell you why they've decided to make that move and that's when they seem most pathetic. Gentlemen, don't bother, that's your business and your responsibility. I don't know what the deal is I've reached with myself, so I don't know why I should be made to feel responsible for the deals you've done with your spouses? I wasn't so sure about all that at the time, and that's why I didn't spit out the insults or the questions on the tip of my tongue. Anyway, this is no news to you, sir, we women always blame lovers for our husbands' infidelities. If I told you the number of times I've heard it said – 'That whore seduced him'. As if they had no control over where they stick it.

I held back the surplus saliva on my teeth and told Him we should call it a day, making an effort so He didn't start hissing traitor out of the corner of his mouth, because He kept his lips sealed tight when he was finding his words. Do you know what it feels like to talk when you're striving to keep the movements of your lips, tongue and throat to a minimum? In reply He began to do something that was typical, rolling his eyes from one side to the other. Whatever you say, He said, though He didn't mean it. Maybe He is one of those who think that when women stammer no they really mean yes and knew that sooner or later He'd be able to slip through a breach in my defences caused by my own doubts. That would have been quite normal, you know? How often had I said no and then switched to yes? The fact is I've met someone and would prefer to concentrate on him because I think it could work out. I don't know if I said that to make Him feel jealous or to convince Him that this time it was for real, that my no was a genuine no.

Then He kept walking around the dining room, laughing, joking, said fine, I'm pleased for your sake. That would be perfect, we would stay as we were, and nobody would lose out. No, you don't understand, I want us to call it a day. I think things can work out well with this guy. I can walk down a street with him, have lunch with him and he can stay and sleep with me on a Saturday night. I can't do any of that with you. No, it's obvious you don't want anything serious with me, you made that clear enough the other day.

I didn't mean that, what I mean is that in your situation you can't even contemplate doing such a thing. Why don't you go home and devote some time to your marriage? That may be your problem, that you don't want to give yourself a second chance, don't want to put in the necessary effort required by a long relationship. You know, I'm no expert, but I don't think it will do you any good if we keep seeing each other. How ridiculous, right, me handing Him advice on how to save his marriage on the basis of a few comments picked up from an afternoon soap. A second chance? How ingenuous, right? Maybe, as I could see He was so on edge, I felt I should lighten his burden. I couldn't really say.

And who is this guy you've met? A guy. Is he good in bed? Shut it. You know what? I'm sure that the way I smiled at Him then was a replica of how I smiled when I started to tell Him about my encounters with other men that He lapped up wanting all the juicy detail.

But this time I wasn't going to tell Him anything about what happened between Mr Impotent and me. In fact, I'd not even been to bed with Mr Impotent. I'd met him one Sunday morning after I'd had a good night's sleep. Not only all night, I had slept almost twenty-four hours, from the moment I got back home from work on Saturday morning. I remember getting up, half asleep, to crunch a few biscuits from a packet I found between

the sheets. And that morning I was sitting on a terrace, sipping
coffee and not believing I could experience a day like that,
through the eyes of someone who was awake, alive and kicking.
A sunny morning into the bargain. Mr Impotent was sitting at
the next table, by himself, reading the newspaper. A tall, thin,
older man, the hair on the back of whose neck was beginning to
recede. You notice people starting to age from the nape of their
necks. I was smiling at everyone in the square, because my back
felt rested, the sun was shining and it was a Sunday. When my
gaze met his, Mr Impotent smiled as well. It happened again
soon after. And again and again until we both started laughing.
Our tables were very close. Now I couldn't tell you what sparked
our conversation, whether it was the sun, the square or his
newspaper. Though that was irrelevant because I was looking
into his eyes very attentively and trying to make sure I didn't
miss a single move made by his lips. All of a sudden I had this
strange turn. It wasn't the usual turn when I felt remorse, which
starts in the groin and moves right inside you, further up, when
the muscles tingled and demanded something be done imme-
diately to fill the vacuum. No, the tingle that Sunday morning
was further up, where my stomach started, and was travelling
in the opposite direction. It came from inside and seemed to be
spreading, to branch out to the rest of my belly, torso, to the
whole of my body. One of those turns that make you feel like
jumping up. And made you laugh.

She walked over to the door to the writer's study. Hey, did
you know there were some clothes in the washing machine?
Yes, of course. But I told you on your first day that I'd see to

the clothes. But when did you put the last lot to wash? I don't know, I don't know, I'll have a look, don't you worry, you just forget it. Let it be for now.

That's right, let it be, with that stink everywhere.

you weren't there

The writer isn't at home today. He must be travelling or have a radio interview or be working in a library. He told her last week, when he gave her a set of house keys, he'd said, I'll be away next week. She's all hot and sweaty when she reaches his house, nervously swings her bags this way and that. At first it's an effort to open the door and she gets panic-stricken at the idea she can't get in, won't be able to clean, and the writer will conclude that he turns his back and she does what she feels like doing and is quite irresponsible. Her pulse is beating fast and she feels queasy in an odd kind of way and felt she might almost fall off the stairs that had no rail. However, in the end she was relieved when she heard the sound of the lock mechanism giving. As soon as she was inside she put her bags down, stood still, and looked down the passage. She can't decide whether cleaning the writer's house when he's not there will be liberating or a drag. While she is thinking about that, her eyes inspect every corner of the house, and she can hear high heels echoing over the pavement stones and into the distance.

She decides to make the space her own, to clean with that freedom of movement she usually has at home, when nobody is watching. She walks over to the writer's sound system and presses the on button. There's a record of classical music in place. So predictable, a writer who listens to classical music. She glances at the collection of CDs next to the system and can find nothing familiar. It's all very odd. She could switch on the telly, put on the afternoon programme she normally watches when she doesn't go to the writer's house, but she thinks that if she does that it will take her longer to finish and she might get to the factory late. No, she decides to find a channel with those pop songs you hear everywhere, she can sing while she cleans. She must remember to change it back. She jots the number down on a scrap of paper so she doesn't forget. She turns the volume up slightly, very slightly. Then looks in the direction of his study and remembers that for sure the writer isn't around. She turns it up even higher until she can hardly hear herself think.

Well, what do you expect, if you're not here, might as well make my work more enjoyable, right? Besides I was particularly happy that day. While I cleaned and danced I was remembering opening my eyes in a dark, dark room. Don't laugh, but swathed in that deep, warm darkness I thought to myself, yes, I'm inside myself. You must think that's strange, I expect. I had slept through the night and so peacefully. It was a room with no cracks in the shutters, no noise of cars in the background or mobiles going off in the silence. I was in Mr Impotent's house in a bed that smelled of lavender. I want to go on waking up like this for the rest of my life, I thought. I would like to be happy like this for the rest of my life and I tried to memorise every detail just in case. If that wasn't happiness... at least nothing could be more comforting than knowing that I was lying in a bed, my skin cradled warmly by the sheets and his body that smelled so good. His body was like Mr Ethereal's, though lighter and longer and his skin was white and delicate. Very hairy, soft skin. I stretched my arm out and coiled it round his waist, all tangled in sheets that, now in the dark, I remembered were high quality white cotton. I thought how in the future I would only need a sprig of lavender to remind me of my first days with Mr Impotent. The pillow was to blame. A pillow for back pain you warm up in the microwave and put over your shoulder. The evening before He'd run to get that pillow when I arrived with my whole week's aches and pains and complaining about the twinges from one muscle. I'd fallen asleep gripping it tight, not letting go. Mr Impotent was such a relief, as if I'd been wanting that all my life. I must be fair, you know, in spite of everything, it was a great relief. When he kissed me for the first time in that Sunday light I simply felt like crying. In fact I'm not so sure I didn't, just a little. Because he was so tender, so respectful, so gentle in the way he held my chin before he put his lips on mine. Just imagine, I'm so soppy. You are very, very pretty, he'd told me, and he said it not as if he was intent on rushing me into bed or persuading me to do something. He said that because it was what he really thought and I simply laughed and turned my eyes to look elsewhere and laugh as if I were a little girl hearing those words for the first time. The day I'm telling you about, that I was remembering when you weren't there, he hugged me and ran his finger along the bottom of my belly that was as soft as those bags of dough balls in the factory fermenting rooms. Hello, love, I heard him say as he turned over and I immediately thought what a breath of fresh air early in the morning. I remembered our candle-lit dinner the night before, like a postcard, him in his apron in the kitchen frying strips of meat, the wine glasses that seemed rimmed with gold. I'd looked at the curtains with embroidered flowery hems, and the snow-white orchid on the kitchen sideboard. A clean, tidy house. I felt at peace.

We got into bed after brushing our teeth and putting our pyjamas on. I told him I hadn't brought any and he gave me a T-shirt. That slightly put me out, I have to say. It was the first time I'd been with a man who only kissed me on the lips, the cheeks, and caressed me behind the ears, and so calm and smiley. It was lovely. I was expecting that to be the first phase, the peaceful beginning to a relationship that was different to the ones I'd experienced up to that point. I thought, tenderness before sex, great! I imagined the follow-up, I imagined him exploring my skin at a similar rhythm, caressing me slowly, turning slowly towards me. I imagined him sticking it in calmly and only when I was sufficiently aroused, and no brusque moves or gestures. I imagined a velvety sex that wasn't invasive, that didn't hurt when it filled me up. I imagined all that while he ran a finger over my lips and smiled. How happy I am! Maybe I hesitated for a moment, wondering whether such gentle sex might not be boring, whether I wouldn't miss the intense thrusting of other men, their bites, and the way they beat my buttocks.

However, we'd washed up together, put on soft background music, drunk a little hot chocolate and soon gone to brush our teeth. That was his idea. He was next to me all the time, a body I could hug, could enjoy and now the tingle wasn't only in my stomach, it was also between my thighs that wanted him. However, he'd just said we should brush our teeth and put our pyjamas on. Are we simply going to sleep? We'd got into bed well wrapped up, him in long trousers and a long-sleeved top and I thought how lucky I was to be with a man who doesn't want to start groping straightaway, who respects you. You can bet sex with him will be very special. I kept hugging him and giving him sloppier and sloppier kisses under the sheets, but he said goodnight and put my head under his chin as if to stop me. I am sure that while he was going to sleep I could still feel my eyes wide open in the dark, and my eyelashes touching the skin on his neck whenever they opened and closed. Good night, love, he repeated, and I thought that maybe it was better like that, that he really loved me, and not just my body…So I gripped the lavender pillow tight.

As the writer isn't there today she will decide what she will do first and second. She always has, but it's such a bother when you are cleaning… Today she will wash his clothes whether he wants her to or not. She goes to the gallery and sees clothes that have been in the washer for days. She opens the round door that makes a clicking sound before the water empties out. The clothes on top are dry and wrinkled, the clothes underneath grey and sticky. She re-shuts the door, fills the little compartment with soap, and softener and ups the temperature to forty degrees. And puts on pre-wash as well, so the clothes are inside a good long while. If she were old-fashioned she'd boil up some water and soak the whole pile of dirty clothes. What an odd guy, what strange ways. She knows the writer won't like what she's doing, that he will complain he told her not to touch his washing, but that's all. If he protests she will tell him she can't work in a house where that nasty smell is always hanging in the air, that however much she cleans the house it never seems clean and always smells as if something is rotting. She's sure that when he walks in and smells how clean it is he will be pleased and won't get angry with her. While the washing machine goes round and round, she does the kitchen, the toilets, sweeps and mops the floor. She mops the floor the way she prefers, barefoot and dancing to music. She thinks how today she can do the study that's always occupied by the writer. He never wants her to, he keeps the door shut, but a little dusting and mopping won't come amiss. She thinks it over and finally decides to open the door. A dark room, with a table at the back strewn with papers. A small room crammed with shelves, and books and papers covering the floor. A high-backed chair facing the table under a shuttered window. She could read things he's written, if he's left them around. That's why she has always tried to avoid private houses, because she's not sure whether she could stop herself from gossiping and prying into the things belonging to the people who live there. And if you find out things about strangers that means you somehow become involved, that they are part of you. She decides she won't, no, she won't read anything by him and goes off to his bedroom. She stretches out to rest for a while. She soon falls asleep.

a dinner, one evening

She says hello to the writer in a voice that's trying to pretend. She almost decided not to come; first, she didn't feel like it, then she took a wrong turning and almost arrived late. I hope you're not annoyed that I washed your clothes: they just smelled so bad. The writer scratches his forehead and says that's fine. You know, people don't understand that cleaning is not simply about cleaning, that it's not something mechanical. I clean one way or another depending on my mood, on how I feel from day to day, and when you weren't here, I suddenly wanted to do a good spring clean. I expect you noticed.

She tucks in her T-shirt, but doesn't stop talking. She turns her shoulder-length hair into a ponytail and keeps talking even when she is gripping the hair-band between her teeth. Did you have a good trip? It was a trip, wasn't it? Yes, of course, it went very well. I brought you this: a tourist guide to the place that I'm sure you've not got. I've done with it so it's all yours. She looks at it and her face lights up and breaks into the broadest smile the writer has ever seen. Thank you so much! She says that while she takes a glance at the book, turns it over, leafs through. You know, it's the expensive kind. It is lovely, she looks at the photos. And she gives the book a hug.

She looks at the writer and wants to hug or kiss him, but just smiles even more broadly. Really thank you so much. So aren't you angry? Why should I be? Because I washed your clothes and dusted and swept your study. I didn't know if you wanted to throw away all the papers strewn across the floor so I put them in the wastepaper basket. No, that's fine, thank you for doing that. Good and thanks for saving my day, because it's one of those weeks that aren't worth remembering. Why do you say that? She's still pressing the book against her chest and swaying slightly, quite unawares. Nothing much, I had a sort of steady boyfriend and have just broken up with him. The one who was your lover? No, I haven't seen Him for ages, I've been with this other guy for a couple of months. Months? I can't believe how time flies… obviously as I only see him on Saturday evenings it seems like we've been together for less time. This one was a *steady* boyfriend. And it didn't work out? I'm not sure, we called it a day but said nothing, but when we said goodbye on Sunday I think it was clear enough that it was going nowhere. Isn't it odd to say goodbye like that, without smashing any plates or a big row or anything at all? Don't you think it's sad that we said goodbye as if we were going to meet up the day after though we knew that was the last we'd see of each other? I always say I understand nothing, but I feel that even more keenly after this episode. So what went wrong? I don't know, everything was perfect, he was so affectionate, very pleasant, very clean and very thoughtful. The kind of man that women in films and series always want, the kind that looks after the small detail, the ones who bring you flowers and say you look great with that new eye shadow or notice you have redecorated your house. He is that kind of man. And what's wrong, didn't you like him enough? No, it's not that ... She shuts up and turns her eyes from the writer leaning on the doorframe unable to contain a smile. I'm embarrassed to tell you. The writer looks at her and says nothing. The fact is he had a very serious... functional problem, if you follow me. Ah, responds the writer. There was no way, in two months! That's why I say it seems we were together for less than two months. Do you think he didn't like me enough? I don't know, do you mean the problem was as simple as that? I just felt so useless every Saturday trying to make it happen. If I tell you any more, I'll dislocate my jaw. She says that before bursting out into laughter and putting a hand over her mouth. I don't know what's wrong with him, you know. How old was he? Forty-eight. Oh, forget it, better look for someone younger, this guy would have died on you far too soon.

I want to invite you to dinner was the message He left me. How did He know that I was no longer with Mr Impotent. Can men smell when you are available? You'll think me way out, but I started to believe that maybe I secreted a different kind of juice when I didn't have a man in particular on my mind, when I could go with whoever. Was I a source of attraction then? You and I, out on the street, all alone, at night, went the next message. I'll take you to a restaurant that you'll just love. But it's Saturday. I know. All right but no fucking. He was quick to reply. I looked in the mirror and saw that the lines around my eyes were getting more and more visible. Or it was the steam from my bath that had made my skin puffy, or lack of sleep or exhaustion, or a combination of

all three. I ran a finger over my arm to check out my skin. It felt
very smooth after I'd rubbed it for a while with my horsehair
glove. I looked at my sad-looking breasts. Were they beginning
to droop or was it premature to be obsessed by such thoughts?
By changes in my weight, maybe. From the day I'd begun going
out with him I'd put on weight; He made me as hungry as an ox.
Then, I'd suddenly lost weight in the months I spent with Mr
Impotent, as if I'd slimmed down from head to toe.

He took me to a town next to mine that evening and occasion-
ally held my hand as we walked along the street. But it wasn't the
kind of hand holding with fingers that slip between your fingers
and press against the inside of the other hand. And you couldn't
feel your small veins pulsating against the soft part of the other
person's hand when you held it tight. And He didn't keep running
his thumbnail against mine. No, what He did was to take my
middle finger between two of his, as if from the outside, as if He
didn't want to make too great an impact.

He introduced me as a friend as he apparently often ate
there. They must have been thinking, she's more than just a
friend. Who takes a friend out to dinner on a Saturday night,
a friend with a swooping neckline and gets as on edge as He
seemed to be? We drank, drank a lot and I soon started to feel
queasy. I found Him good to be with, even more attractive and
interesting. He could be mine. Did I just want Him to myself?
Shaving in my bathroom day in day out? What would He see in
me if He had me all the time? Maybe He'd treat me like his wife
and look for another woman to brighten up his weekdays? I'd
always worried about how He managed it so his wife didn't find
out? You bet she knew because of the smell, let alone anything

else. I could always detect when He'd fucked his wife before He came to me. Which didn't happen very often. The fool, I thought as I heard Him talking as if He were talking to himself. She really is a fool if she doesn't fuck her husband. Doesn't she know that a daily fuck is what keeps a couple together? You leave a trace of yourself on the other person and the other women can smell it. That's why when a man has a partner but they don't do it very often it's more likely he'll have a bit on the side. Don't you reckon? Look, right now I could make a list of the men I've been with who were in exactly that situation.

I was cheerful in his car and I turned the volume up on the singer's heart-rending voice. Her songs were so sad. But I began to dance to a different rhythm, as if I was in fact listening to frantic music in a club. When we were outside the door He said goodnight. No, please don't leave. I looked at Him not at all sarcastically or ironically, really meaning what I said, maybe for the first time… Why don't you come in for a moment?

Once inside we flopped down on the rough carpet in my dining room. I thought how I'd missed that familiar body, that a body that spends so long with yours is not the same as a body you spend twenty minutes with on the train or in a dermatologist's consultancy. It was a teeny bit mine, you know? It was nice to feel that warmth. We made love then, at least that's what I remember. I remember stopping to think in an alcoholic haze and telling myself: we are making love at this very moment.

When we finished He wrapped his legs around me and I rested my head on his back. We stayed like that for a few minutes until He cleared his throat and said He had to go. What? I have to go. At any other time I'd have snapped at Him you do whatever *you want to and got into bed without saying goodbye. But I was very drunk. I thought you could sleep over with me… I felt my knees were on fire, I was missing the skin that had rubbed off on the carpet when I'd said stay, please. Just this one night for me. One night when we sleep together. Aren't you always saying that you would like to sleep with me one night? I'm sorry, I can't. And here am I playing out the most clichéd role in history, crying like I'd not cried for a long time, as I'd never cried in front of him, maybe recalling that heartrending voice on the car radio. Just today, please, I don't want to sleep by myself today. You did say you could, just now, you did say you could. No, I said we could have dinner together. I told my wife I had a dinner with people from work, but it's getting too late now. So why did you do all that? Why? So we could be together on a Saturday night. Isn't that what you wanted? No, I want nothing from you. Do you know why? Do you know why? Because you are a bastard, a son of a bitch and a shit that mistreats the women He likes. In fact, you're just in love with yourself, you don't love anyone else. Because when you said you loved me you only said that to make sure you'd get a lay, because you are a coward running away from his real problems. You know what? You can clear out of my life forever. I don't want to see you again. Got that? Never ever.*

As I said all that I began to note a queasy feeling rising through me. After He'd left and shut the door, not saying a word to deny my accusations, I rushed to the bathroom and started to throw up. Time and again as if I was bringing up weeks of food. When I thought I couldn't vomit anymore, I started all over again. Until I was exhausted, with my arms around the toilet bowl, feeling I had vomited myself up.

THIS IS A KIND OF THERAPY

You, sir, have no idea what is going through the head of a person stepping out into the street to find somebody to fuck. Lots and lots in a very short space of time. Your body insists you do it, your skin surges over your body in giant waves, your nostrils flare wide open to smell out your prey. When I go out into the street in this state I feel I'm like an animal crossing the threshold, I feel I'm changing into a wolf running to hunt its food. But it's more than that, much more. I'm out to get a body and couldn't care less what kind. A big man, an old man or young man, a young boy or wild beast. Sometimes I've thought I'd be happy with an animal, a dog, a cat I could feel panting and wriggling in my hands. A rat rubbing against my palm. A piece of pulsating flesh and blood would be just right on a day like that when I feel I am more animal than human. You know what it is? It's my body rebelling against me. It's my body telling me it's had enough of the kind of hole I'm stuck in, enough of being in limbo. My body wouldn't stand so much if I didn't force it to. When it's tired after working night and day, after not sleeping, and stuffing to the point of being sick, or not eating to the point of inhabiting an empty shell, it says enough is enough and makes its own way into the street. You have to believe this, when I come here I'm not myself, it's not itself, we're not together. That's how I can go out looking for live bodies to gobble up. That's how I can turn into somebody else and do what I wouldn't do if I ever stopped to think. And all to placate a cry, a cry that always comes from inside asking loudly: 'Anyone there?' And then vanishes and leaves me with a body to slice.

You have to help me, really only you can help me. Ever since men first started to look at me I've been unable to resist the call of their desire. Men are like pistols aimed at me. You can't leave them all horny like that. But none of that works now, I don't get the hots anymore in a lavatory or in a bar, I can't let them touch me on the train or give a blow job to a guy I've only just met. I don't know why I can't do what I've always done, I don't know what I have to do to get rid of all my tensions. Can you see what my back is like? Do you realize how inhuman all this is? Don't make judgements; it's not right. I need to do it, I need to fuck one way or another. Today is a day in the month when my body cries out for contact with another body, whatever the body. Can't you see how I need to do it? When a woman's in that state, going out in search of a body is like an urge that comes out of the blue, as if every single muscle was raring to go. That's not how it's always worked, right? Men used to be the ones going out in search of prey, right? But you know what? I don't want to be anybody's prey, anybody's victim. Why can they do that and not me? Why do they sometimes take fright when I take the initiative, when I make the move to deal with their desires? Because I might be ignorant of lots of things, but I always know when a man wants me. Since before I'd become a woman, a day when I looked at myself in the mirror and was wearing a tight-fitting white jersey. I could see my breasts standing out because the jersey was a kind of cashmere and I was pleased it looked so nice. However, a neighbour much older than me was looking out of a window, dressed as if about to go on military service, and I saw he was looking at me very differently. I could read in his eyes that he guessed I'd become more of a woman. He upset me and shattered the image I'd created of myself in that white jersey. I've been able to identify that kind of glance ever since. Do you think I'm being presumptuous? Well, I'm not; I know what I'm talking about. You know when a man wants you and how he will do it to you. It's been far too long since my body trembled, or I felt one of those shudders that makes you forget everything else. Weeks. No, months. I didn't do anything with Mr Impotent. We just caressed. What was wrong with him? What was it? A man I didn't even give a single wretched erection. Or rather only one I never told you about, towards the end of our affair. We were having dinner and he stared at me hard. Did you know that men can also guess what kind of lover you will be? They know exactly what you're going to ask for. I think Mr Impotent never got a hard-on because he could see only too clearly that I liked energetic lovers. I know that's the case because he did something very odd when we were dining. He gave me a piece of food on a fork and simply stared hard at me with his fork on my lips, on my upper lip, right, it was pleasant feeling that hard, cold thing on body flesh that is so soft, and he soon started to press down. Very gradually, as if testing the terrain. I loved it and half-opened my mouth to let him continue as long as he wanted. He kept pressing harder, just looking at my mouth, not my face, as if from that moment only he and my lips existed in that room. He kept pressing and I shut my eyes hoping that any second he would break the skin and blood would spurt out. You know, don't you, that blood from the lips is redder than blood from the rest of the body? But he never pierced me and I was left longing on the brink. He suddenly snapped out of it, when I threw my head back because I was liking it so much. I am sure he got a hard-on then, but he acted as normal and stopped. And when I was with him the other day everything was so low-key I didn't manage to forget myself, didn't do it, quite the contrary, in fact. That's why I now need someone to dominate me rigorously, to whip me if necessary, to strap me down and do whatever he wants. Until I'm out of it and can't feel my body. You can't imagine how annoying it is when my body is so tense, how it's really bad. Look, I think I'm getting red blotches everywhere, my skin's flaking and strips are coming away of their own accord. Yes, I know they aren't really, but my skin is hurting. I have tried to do it by myself. Making little cuts, say. I've taken a knife and tried to cut a piece out of my thigh, from the inside flesh that's a shade darker just before you reach my sex. I think it's a blemish that's spreading and I'd like to remove it. I've sometimes been rubbed in that spot, and I can tell you nothing gives more pleasure than that, it's even better than when they rub your cunt. Please help me, I can't stand anymore of this. I can't go out after a man because I can't fool myself into not feeling it's nasty and I don't want to ring other lovers I've had because I hate them. Please, only you can help. Obviously, you are going to tell me to stop, to forget about men for a while. Is that the only solution you can offer?

This is unsettling me. See if you can understand and help me to understand myself. I know it might seem very unlikely at first sight but now I keep a careful watch on myself after going so long without a man. I'm walking down a street when a man suddenly gives me a glance. Or it's me at the factory with all that water splashing off my plastic overall, my sweat mixed up with squirts of disinfectant and my face covered by a mask. My nostrils trapped inside green paper. And a man appears whose desire I can detect, because I know when a man desires me, I told you as much, it's no longer a secret I need to check out, yet this knowledge doesn't incite me to take a single step towards him. His desire slips right off me. Maybe because the secret is out now. I used to have to investigate in some way because I didn't believe they liked me, but now I know. As I've not had another body near mine since that Saturday night when I vomited endlessly and decided, following your advice, to give up sex for a while, I now have no choice but to be alone with my body.

What should I do with it? What do you reckon I should do with this piece of live flesh I feel is mine, though it isn't, that often seems alien, that I hate as fiercely as I can? You don't

believe it? That you can hate your own body? Well, you can, I
detest mine, I feel it's so terrible and disgusting I simply want
out. No, it's not about looks. It's something else. I feel every
corner is straining, my shoulders, the middle of my back, this
strange, lumpy wall that supports my lungs. Have you ever
touched that part of your body? You just need to press two
fingers under your ribs until you can poke between two front
ribs here and you'll find it is a slippery wall with a life of its
own, like the body. I can't control this part of me, it shakes
when I feel things, when I'm angry, when I'm excited. It's an
awkward bit of flesh, you know, made of filaments covered in
knots, like a diary of everything I feel and never say, never
mention. The other day, after insulting Him as strongly as I
could I thought this perpendicular piece of flesh was going
to burst, I imagined it splattering everywhere and strewing
my place with everything I'd not said that had accumulated
in the entrance to my stomach. Maybe that was why I ran to
the lavatory and vomited until I'd emptied everything out, so
as not to soil the things around me. Afterwards, like an empty
bottle waiting to be filled, I thought my torso was whistling
like the wind and I simply burst into tears. Don't you think it
odd that it's often very difficult to cry? How come we can't do
so whenever we want, at anytime of the day? It was a Saturday
and I had a peaceful night's sleep.

But that was days ago and you, sir, don't want to help me,
you told me to stop, to give up men for a while and you don't
seem to understand I have no other pleasures in life. I would
like to go back to how I was before thinking I must make the
most of life, in case I went into the street and was knocked

over by a car and couldn't experience any more orgasms, but do you know what I'm like now? Well, I can do none of that now and it's as if I was on a hamster's treadmill and could only go round and round. No men there, I've none now, but the more days that go by when I don't give my body up to one, the guiltier I feel. As if I'd an obligation towards them I was neglecting. Don't you see, my body is no use for anything else? Yes, naturally, you'll say that's not the case, but what do you know about that, shut up here night and day? What do you know about life? I don't know why I'm taking any notice of you and not just going with men again. I follow the advice of a man who spends the whole day shut up between four walls typing out stories he's invented on a computer. You know nothing about men, you don't know how they need me. But then their desire no longer sets me on fire and you know what? I can no longer figure out what my desire is all about.

There are other things I ought to tell you too, however strange it might seem, my body disgusts me, takes up too much space in this world. That's why I look for ways to control it, to make sure it doesn't overflow, as if it were a liquid spilling over the edge of a container. If you like, I can tell you about the things I do so my body doesn't bother me as much, to scold it until it's worked out its guilt for being so body-like in the middle of this world.

Eating. There are the pleasures of eating, the sensual savouring of tastes in my mouth, but, to tell you the truth, I forgot about that long ago. Food usually soothes this restless filament under my lungs. But don't get me wrong, it's not simply about over-eating a little. If it is really going to work as I say, to enable me to forget my body, I have to stuff myself until I can no longer feel, until I am so full I think my food is up to my gullet, until I'm so busy digesting I can no longer feel any irritation in any part of my belly. And what if I tell you that I can never eat too much rubbish? You know, when I'm struck by that bolt that insists I be whipped immediately, be strapped down and be subjected to the will of somebody else and dispense with my own, the only way I can find to repress that is by devouring things I wouldn't normally eat, that I think are bad for you, and hardly noticing the taste. Fatty things, full of sugar, even better if they're cheap, and poorly prepared and cooked. I'll give you an example: one day I went to the supermarket next to my place and bought a whole pack of hamburgers. Remember how I worked in a supermarket packing meat? I know perfectly well that hamburgers are made from twice-recycled meat long past its sell-by date. So I bought two packs of four, mayonnaise, ketchup, that bland bread that's full of sugar and guess what I did? Just imagine: first, four whole hamburgers, with loads of chips I just shoved in the pan, lots of sauce, and I *stuffed* the lot down me as quickly as I could, squatting on the dining-room carpet. Then four more. How lovely, I told myself, but I can tell you it wasn't really pleasure from the food, the enjoyment of a good meal, every bite I took felt like somebody was chasing me, like a blast of pain, a whiplash hitting my groin. Finally I felt at peace with that putrid mix of meat and that sweet sauce seeping first into my mouth, then my throat, then my stomach, flooding me because I'd taken such a big bite, with my thighs bared on the rough material, stretching my head back, ketchup and mayonnaise trickling down my chin and neck to my breasts, I finally felt at peace. I bet you must be imagining that the worst was yet to come, when I wolfed the lot or couldn't go on and it was as if the whole world had piled into my belly which was about to burst and destroy everything. I've already mentioned the seventh-floor effect, well, eating like that produces exactly the same outcome. The same hangover that compulsive sex gives you. And you can't imagine how difficult it is to rid yourself of that sense of being stuffed. However much I would have liked to try, I've never been able to force myself to throw up. And that has its own consequences, you know? I've always admired bulimics: they inflict harm on themselves eating tons of food that's bad for them but then they know how to rid their bodies of it so it's no longer part of them. I don't, I keep the lot inside and balloon out. Men have the same impact, as if I kept packing them inside me. How on earth do you vomit up a lover?

I've sometimes been so angry after one of these fridge attacks that I've rushed to ditch all the food there, to get rid of anything my brain might think harmful. But you know what? It makes no odds, I always manage to find a way to get rubbish to feed my body. You'd be amazed the lengths I can go to when desperation sends me into a spin. On a bank holiday, when everything was shut and I'd cleaned the kitchen, I got out of bed with a desire to eat anything I could lay my hands on. I rummaged in all the cupboards and found nothing, absolutely nothing. I was anxious, frantic, wanted to relieve that tingle in my stomach and grabbed the only edible item in the kitchen, a packet of flour. I didn't know what to do with it, since I had no eggs, yeast, or sugar. I was desperate, had the shakes and poured the flour into a bowl and added water. I stirred it as long as I could and fried the sticky, white paste in a pan. Then I stood there with a dish full of the stuff and swallowed it all, and it was tasteless, it tasted more of death than life and each mouthful scalded my tongue.

Do you think I should change my job? Naturally, you don't answer me, as usual you give me that look that says nothing at all, waiting for me to answer my own question. Well, you know, what can I say, you're not much help. By the way, do you know you've got ants in your kitchen? I've got the moths more or less under control, I see the odd one now and then but it soon sticks to that nasty paper I hung up inside the cupboard doors. If one does appear I can tell you it won't escape me. However, the ants have cut a path from behind a crack in the kitchen top to the sink. Please do me a favour and don't leave any crumbs of food anywhere, or else they'll never go and I'll have to remove them with a duster and I *hate* doing that.

Well, you know, I often think that this cleaning business is probably a waste of time, I come here, sweep, mop, vacuum, dust, clean the windows, but what's the point if everything gets dirty again in no time at all? And don't think I'm complaining about you dirtying the place, it's just that the world is dirty in itself: bits fall off the walls, the ceiling, your skin, your hair, we all spread bits around over time quite unawares, we keep paring down and flaking like everything around us. You know, that wall you think will always be the same never will be.

But if I mention changing jobs, it's because I'm starting to get sick of cleaning. And especially cleaning at night, what a complete waste of time. Who on earth notices in the dark whether a pizza production line is more or less clean? Of course, people do, and even more so when the biologist comes by with his little sheets of paper to do tests, who tells us if that's enough or not, if we need to hose a bit more. You know, I don't get it, and the more I clean the less I get it. I get angry, right? I get very angry when the cleaning gets on top of me and I don't know where to start or where to finish. You'll think that's odd given that I've spent half my life doing this, but I promise you there are days I just feel like giving up, as if I'd learned nothing in all that time, as if it was my first time and I felt completely useless, clueless, totally at a loss. I just want to run away and never go back to cleaning. That's when I feel most trapped.

And I walk off, you bet I do, walk off to the factory lavatories to try and forget I've work to do, I have a thousand different ways to distract myself, I seek refuge in a hidden corner nobody knows about and try to make time go by without cleaning. And even though you won't believe me, that's when I feel saddest and most disappointed with myself. It's as if I'd left my house, my self, and was depriving myself of the pleasure of doing the work I want to do. Not that you'll believe this either, this *is* the work I want to do, *is* what I like and what gives meaning to my life, even if nobody wants to clean, as you know. Some people think it's humiliating, they think it's work for people who don't deserve anything better. Shop assistants at counters show off to customers, fawn all over them. Everybody thinks that cleaning is for rejects, but I can tell you that when I don't have a mop to hand I feel sadder than ever. Maybe you don't believe me, right? Don't worry, if you want to think I'm crazy it doesn't bother me, think away.

I tell you, I'm so sad when I'm in a corner of the factory, behind a wall of pizza pallets all jammed together, biting my nails with my mask under my chin and anger welling in my throat. I keep repeating to myself you can't do it, you can't, you don't know how, you're useless, slow, witless, while from afar I watch women wielding the power hoses and driving the remains of the food into the drain, then sweeping up with a shovel. Know what I think at such moments? Know what? Terrible envy at seeing them do it so easily and not wondering whether they should or shouldn't be doing it, whether they are doing it well or not. It's strange, you know, when you stop yourself doing something that in fact nobody else is stopping you from doing.

And now it's no different here. You must see, right, that it's much better to clean by day rather than by night? Well, you know, I usually look forward to coming here. But when I'm beset by these doubts about whether I should be cleaning or not, whether I'm really good enough to do what I like doing, or really deserve to earn my living doing what I feel like doing, then when I come to your place I start wanting to rush off and never come back. But I am here and I can't stop myself, even though you won't believe me, I need to clean rather than to live.

How can that be? Well, it's very simple, when I clean it's a pleasure quite unlike any other, it's a thrill caused by the fact I'm doing something that's useful to me and to others. How is it useful to me? I don't know exactly but the moment I begin to introduce some order, to remove the remnants I mentioned before, leaving it all as if no time has passed, or as if life wasn't in fact very disorderly, as if the world wasn't, in some way I do think I've changed this world a tiny bit. But I will tell you something I've not told anyone else: the most pleasurable part of cleaning isn't the wellbeing I bring other people, it's the wellbeing I bring myself. And that wellbeing comes with the feeling that I have some power over things outside of me, but most of all it's the impression that I'm spreading myself into every corner. Don't give me that bemused expression, it makes sense: look at your apartment, look at the dirt spread everywhere. When I finish cleaning today you know what will be spread round every corner? Well, I can tell you: *I* will be. I can see you don't understand, but it's obvious enough: I put my whole body into my cleaning, and this is the way I relate to the world, I surrender and shield myself from everything I can't understand. When I clean and ferret in every corner of your living room, I am an uptight woman suddenly letting go, pouring and splashing everywhere. That's what I'm like when I clean, I belong to this world and this world becomes part of me.

Yet again I'm in flight from Him and taking refuge in your house. Yes, I know, I should have sorted this business by now ... But don't think that today's one of those days when He keeps ringing and I find it hard to say no. No, not today, no way is He chasing. In fact, He's not even rung me. I got up racked with pain and not knowing what to do with my body. My first thought was a fantastic afternoon of sex. Or the frenzied movements to orgasm that I'm not sure amount to sex. The movement of the flesh and bones that support my back underneath, from the ground upwards. Until I forget they are all connected. Until the sinews joining them together suddenly fall away when I come. Yes, today I seriously contemplated ringing Him, my fingers throbbed with terrible longings. Go on, dare to, I told myself, as if phoning Him was a challenge. We're still on the hamster's treadmill, you see. Why is it a challenge? Because I am a woman: women don't phone men. Even though people think times have changed, I can tell you there are few women who take the first step. It's part of the game. We reckon that if we ring a man he'll wonder what we want from him, what are we after? But I can tell you this isn't the case with me. He'd be delighted if I rang Him, if only to say hello. He makes life easy for me; when I ring Him He does the rest. I only have to say hello and He's already asking if I want him to come. He never asks why I've rung and I often put the phone down without spelling out why I have rung. Of course it's obvious, but sometimes I'm not at all sure if what is obvious to me is the same as what's obvious to Him. There are days I would ring just to have lunch, to spend a while together, but we both know only too well what our meetings always lead to. I've sometimes warned Him, have said come but we won't fuck today. And you've guessed, haven't you? The moment I say that, I can see neither of us believes a word of it. It's like a vice with us two.

How miserable, believe me, all alone at home, about to send a message and fuck the whole thing up. He's not bothered me from the day I puked everything up, but you know, don't you, that if I ring Him I will undo all the progress I've made since then? I'm tempted to turn back, and meet up with Him again or with other men. Don't think I can't now see how they seek me out, demand my body, but it's as if I am paralyzed, I can't go forward or back. I still feel I'm on a treadmill not of my own choosing. I'd never seen it like that until now. Believe me, I'm proud of everything I've done, but I see myself a little differently now.

It's the bother, right? The bother my body causes upsets me all the time, from the moment I started thinking about all of them and telling you about every affair, as if I was telling you when in fact I'm telling myself. When I was living through those encounters with my lovers I thought I was the happiest, most liberated woman in the world. Liberated more than anything else because I succeeded in doing what few women in the factory could do, that is, release myself from the humdrum and concentrate solely on pleasure. So the more men the merrier, the more peculiar the circumstances the better, the more daring the affairs the better. Now as I remember them I think other feelings were mixed up with that sense of victory over archaic rules established by those around me. But I really can't tell you what irritates me most about them. Maybe I'm angry with all those men because they didn't know how to give me what I wanted, even though I didn't know what that was, and in fact still don't. I'm one big mess and this mass of flesh is to blame, but I am clear about one thing and have been all this time that I've been going out with men: what they wanted from me. I've always known what that was and perhaps that's why they always chase after me. At the end of the day, you're a man and must know, all they want is sex. Don't look at me like that because mine's the voice of experience. How many men have I counted as having passed through me? Loads, and not one, not a single one has wanted anything from me that wasn't sex. How do I know? Well, you know, it's very easy, even when they said they wanted to love me, wanted me to be a friend or whatever, that they really did, when I provoked them they never said no to sex. I tested them out, right? I'd like to have proved that one of them wasn't interested in my sex, but they all came after that and never said no if I offered myself. Yes, obviously, Mr Impotent with that brotherly warmth of his never wanted it, but it's obvious that guy had a serious hang-up.

Naturally, you'll now say we get what we look for and that if I always look for men interested in sex I'll inevitably find them, but you won't deny there isn't a sameness about men today. There are all kinds? Yes, maybe, but at this point in time those worth considering are either spoken for or else not my kind.

Do you want me to let you in on another secret? Men so get up my nose that all I can do is try to get out of myself and forget them. I want to forget them because I'm so angry. No, I don't know why, but I am and I realize the more annoying I find them the more annoying I find myself. But I often find a more acceptable solution than stuffing down all the food I have at hand. Can you guess what it is? It's doing exactly the opposite, a diet so strict it hardly gives me time to think. I sleep as much as I can during the day, get up and drink a cup of tea with saccharine or a diuretic infusion, and off I go to the factory. I avoid the breaks for dinner by running the cleaning of one line into the next and maybe chew gum. Yes, I'm used to chewing gum all night so as not to smell. Did you know we give off odours when we're slimming? The body's evaporating and disappearing through every orifice in solid and liquid form as well as air. I should know, I'm shrinking on this diet. When I get home exhausted and my thoughts swing this way and that, slowly, as if thinking in my sleep, in slow motion, I look in the mirror before I reluctantly swallow any warm liquid. An infusion with a laxative pill, but sometimes I feel so dead I don't have time for that and simply swallow tasteless hot water from the tap to silence my rumbling stomach.

Then I sleep and just want to sleep forever more. No, don't you think that I'm going to commit suicide, that's silly, just sleep until I exit my body. Don't you think that would be a brilliant move? If only I could live without my body, loan it out for a while or pawn it for the duration or burn it in a container. Shred it and just be myself, with no hang-ups. Well, I tell you, shrinking like this is a slight step in that direction. I feel I am light, if not ethereal, and though you might not think so, I'm happy like this, taking up less space, not bothering others or myself. You know, the first things to shrink are my breasts and that makes me feel less of a woman. I really am happy, ignore the tears, they are tears of joy. No doubt you'll tell me that what I have to do is love my body, that I am my body and it is vital to learn to love it. Listen, just shush, sir, and please do me a favour and pay some attention to these ants that have invaded your kitchen.

It's shit being a woman. I don't say that idly, women are a

disaster zone. We women make more filth than men. I know, everyone thinks quite the opposite because men are usually sloppier and in general couldn't care less about cleanliness, but that's just on the surface. Should I tell you why? Well, just think, if we simply focus on bodies and not on what we do with them, if we simply think about the dirt we involuntarily leave around I can prove that men are cleaner. It's a matter of fact, the way our bodies are built is to blame. Men don't give off as many fluids as we do. When they piss, pee doesn't stick to their penises. A little does, maybe, but it's further from the body than ours, and, yes, they do ejaculate, but when they do so they shoot it away, right, they don't dirty themselves. That's why I've always reckoned men's bodies are cleaner than women's. Everything stays inside us and we can't let it out without dirtying ourselves. And we also secrete more stuff, right? I tell you, it *is* shit being a woman. I've been trying to hide the fact for eighteen years, month after month, pretending not to be a woman; it seems so pointless. What *is* the point in being a woman?

You say you don't see it's so obvious that women secrete more than men? Well, what about vaginal fluid, that nobody can find a reason for? An ejaculation leaves the body as the result of a specific process, there is cause and effect, but, however many theories there may be, no one has managed to explain the purpose of vaginal fluids. Yes, you can say that most tend to appear when you're aroused, but even that's not entirely true. You are sometimes highly aroused and so dry that your skin ends up sore. Then there's the business of the days of the month and one day your knickers are full of a sticky substance you can pick up in your fingers and see how thick, almost solid it is, and the next day the fallout is so liquid you think you've pissed yourself.

And then, obviously, there is blood, the most repulsive secretion imaginable. From the time that started I've thought the world, the whole universe, is terribly unfair. It's a punishment, I've already told you as much. I don't know, I can't fathom why other women throughout the world take it so naturally, so in their stride, because I get depressed whenever it comes. If they told me of a cure to get rid of it, I'd sign up for it right now. The worst of it is that my blood flows so plentifully, as if I was leaking blood and dying. I sometimes feel as if something was coming out, as if part of my insides was being pulled out. And you know what? I have seen how it is part of me: solid clots often, really solid stuff, and when I see that in the water in the toilet bowl I feel queasy and think that periods are just a kind of disease.

Then there are other drawbacks. Do you know what has always frightened me most in this world? That I might be leaking bloodstains somewhere, that I'm not in control of my period, that it's soaking my tampon, my sanitary towel, my knickers and seeping through my trousers and staining the surface where I'm sitting. What if I were to tell you that it worries me so much that on the days I have my period I only sit down in your house? Don't you think this is nature being unfair?

At any rate, this unfairness has dragged me back into the light of day. How? Well, the other day I was up on one of the machines that distributes cheese, mopping the hidden crannies, when I fainted. Just like that, like an old-fashioned fainting fit, I turned round to say something to a workmate and fell on top of her like a lump of lead. Luckily I wasn't very high up. And luckily it didn't happen when we were cleaning with pressure hoses. You know, it can be a major catastrophe if the condenser on the hose gets detached. If that piece of metal hits you, you are dead.

To tell you the truth, I wasn't that sick. It was as if I'd suddenly fallen asleep, as if someone had snapped their fingers, and said sleep. Luckily it was that lady, an older woman who's always laughing and keeps herself to herself. She caught me as I fell and I brought her down as well, though we were both unscathed. Then they took me to hospital. By then I was fine and told them not to bother, but they insisted on doing so. In fact, the older lady said don't worry, you're all right but better if they do a check-up. Would you believe me if I told you that they made me feel so relaxed and comfortable it was like being back at home? She stayed with me for the rest of the night and looked at me and asked if I ate well, if I looked after myself properly. Dear, if you live by yourself, perhaps nobody ever tells you, but you do need to look after yourself. I glanced at her and said nothing. I was so exhausted and she ran her hand over my hair and tidied it behind my ear. When she did that, combing me like a young child, I suddenly felt all the woes in the world and started to cry as I'd never cried before. Just because she'd stroked my hair.

It's true that lovers of sex for sex's sake caressed me. It's inevitable, your bodies meet, you squeeze an arm and you squeeze a neck. If our sexes could operate independently maybe we might dispense with bodies and chance caresses. But I'll tell you a secret: caresses of that kind don't touch the same places as caresses inspired by love and affection. The skin on the receiving end is different to your normal skin or the skin that friends and those you love touch. When I'm with my lovers, what comes, what surfaces on my body is skin like armour-plating, skin able to resist anything, from gestures of tenderness to the beatings I long for, the bites or whiplashes, so they don't hurt me. It's like the green plastic uniform at the factory that covers everything else and off which sluices water, soap, disinfectant and scraps of food that come out of the machines as we clean them. I'll tell you another secret: it's not true they don't leave any mark on that temporary skin just because of the sex I'm having with them. Do you understand? Later on, when they've gone, when I'm alone, I realize that what I thought was armour-plating was in fact my skin. That's how this layer of scars and teeth marks was formed. Do you see? It is a map that could easily deliver up the names and dates of those who provoked them. Maybe not every name, but I do remember their faces, and, above all, their smells. I'll tell you something else: the armour-plating I thought was of my own making is plating that gradually poisons you.

Today I felt the rot in my body was pursuing me again. Tired, after starving for days, not having managed a wink of sleep the whole day, by mid-afternoon I thought I was going crazy. Really crazy, I tell you. What was it like? Well, you know, I closed my eyes for a while on the sofa, but woke up terrified because although I was still asleep I thought I could see ants climbing up my legs. And when I woke up, I began to see the men in my life putting in an appearance, one by one, and setting up in my house. You can imagine the distress... I began to recreate their caresses, their jerking, blows, whip-lashes, kisses, the neck grabbing and know what? First one was touching me, then two at once. It was so real at times I thought I'd gone back to them, that I'd abandoned the cease-fire you, sir, advised and for a few moments I cried tears of rage inside. I kept asking myself why, why can't I get off that treadmill, and my body hurt more than ever. I found myself in the middle of the dining room, banging my knees down with all my might on the ribbed carpet, my skin was stinging, peeling off. And no pleasure, I can assure you, sadness choked me, let me cry only if I threw my head back with tears that streamed over and into my ears. By then it wasn't just two men grabbing me, it was three, four, ten, fifteen, all sharing out scraps of my skin, all with their separate hard-ons, penetrating me everywhere, even in places where I had no holes. Sounds strange, doesn't it? Well, it wasn't, they were trying to penetrate my elbow or knee, tried to penetrate me with their bites and there was a moment when I thought they wanted to carve me up between them. Each of them clinging to his bit, pulling my skin as hard as he could, so taut, so taut it almost ripped to shreds.

I couldn't stand it anymore, right? Not just the tautness but the chaos of those bodies in mine. Who were they? How many were there? What did they want from me? While they pulled me like a sheet about to rip, by the arms, feet, neck, ears, cunt-lips, soft skin inside my thighs, each fold, while they were doing all that, I thought that a whole swarm of ants was advancing over my toes. And that's your fault, sir, you don't take the ant problem seriously, you say they don't do any harm, don't pass on disease and the best we can hope for is learn to cohabit with them. And look, the other day I had to use a duster to get rid of them. The sight of my duster full of tiny corpses was disgusting. I find them even more disgusting when they come after me in my dining room. In the end I couldn't stand being stretched out so long by myself. Nobody can save you from yourself when you are alone, you know how true that is. And if it is sad to cry out of despair, I can tell you it's even sadder when you do so alone.

I began to bawl at them to let me be, I shouted, clear off, you bastards, leave me in peace, but they laughed, can you imagine? They laughed and repeated things they'd said to me when they were with me, you must think about us two, you are very lovely, end of operation, I sucked your blood and it was *riquísima*, I love you. All their voices had fused into one and I didn't know how to get away, what with the sobbing that was doubling me over and my whole body feeling as if they were still pulling it taut. They looked at me and laughed as if to say I belonged to all of them, you are ours, they seemed to be shouting, looking at each other as if in cahoots. I tried to forget them by recalling the corpses of the ants between my fingers, but they were on the march. Know what I did in the end? Don't be shocked, by this stage you know I'm rather peculiar, but what could I do if I couldn't escape from so many people? There was a moment when I thought I liked that scene, I let myself melt into the bodies and know what? I was really like one of them, and belonging to that gang of men as if I belonged to the world. However, I suddenly remembered them all, not as individuals, but as bodies and I couldn't stand them being only bodies. I realized the skin I had adopted for them wasn't so much the sex for sex's sake skin I'd thought and I felt I was going down a path of no return. If only I could ring someone and at the very least tell him, but who do you think will want to listen to this tale of hallucinations? So as I couldn't find a way out I went into the kitchen and grabbed a knife, a small, very sharp one I always used. I sat back on the carpet with my legs spread-eagled and rested the knife on the skin on the inside of my thighs, which soon yielded it was so soft. I wanted to press it down gradually, not cutting myself yet, though in fact nobody would have thought I wasn't. And know what, while I made that move, knowing full well I was quite capable of taking it further, rather than enjoying the experience, I again saw the path of no return, the path that separated the healthy from the mentally sick. Yes, true, maybe I was totally crazy by the time I reached this point, but I could see that path, you know? I could see they were that path as they stretched my body and laughed, as if I wasn't there. I wanted to flee even further, I said go on, cut yourself, and as I thought about it, I felt my breath wasn't mine, that I'd run out. So what? If you're not hurting anyone, go on, cut yourself, cut yourself as much as you want right now, relish the feeling even more, pour salt on your wounds and you'll feel the pleasure gnawing at you, you'll have gone beyond every boundary of pain.

I was so close to doing all that I still find it hard to accept I stepped back from the brink. What was it that made me? What was the precise moment when I said enough, enough, enough, shouting as loudly as I could, when I got up and threw the knife in the direction of the kitchen? I don't really know, but I do vaguely remember putting my trainers on in a rush and going out. I almost did so barefoot. I went out and broke into a run. When was the last time I did that? Don't think it was one of those races you run at a brisk pace for the purpose of exercise, what I did was completely different. You know how I'm always telling you I'm in flight from myself? Well, starting to run was like running away from myself, shouting, arms outstretched, accelerating with every step. When I reached the riverbank, a bridge, I gripped the rail, leant over, gazed at the water and started to scream as I'd never done before. A mute, animal scream, and one that wasn't so deep, surfaced amid my screams, but it was an inhuman rage that comes from somewhere unknown. I was outside, like that, for a long time, just imagine. First, sobbing endlessly. For a moment I thought I couldn't sob or shout anymore. I'm not exactly sure when the tear-filled cry of rage and sadness turned into loud laughter. Yes, you see, just like people who are unhinged, I stopped sobbing and started laughing, sitting on that timber bridge. Do you know why I was laughing? As I was running all the blood in my body had splattered everywhere, and know what? For the first time I felt it was *my* body throbbing, that it belonged to me. I felt every scrap of me was tingling. You don't know how happy I was. I could feel my body and not because others were to blame, I could feel it because of myself, thanks to me.

Then I came here, though it wasn't yet daytime and you, sir, opened the door and I went straight into the kitchen, if you remember. Do you know why? Because I suddenly felt ants were the nicest species on earth and they no longer disgusted me. Those tiny sexless creatures no longer bothered me.

The doctors say I need to rest. That I fainted because of a mixture of tiredness and lack of iron and some other substance in my blood. They enquired about my sleeping and eating habits and I felt like I was in an exam. You know, I'm on sick leave right now, but if you don't mind I'll continue coming here, I don't think the hours here will do me any harm. I just have to keep quiet about them. The doctor recommends I take it easy and don't immediately return to the night shift because I'll only have another fainting fit and in my case that is dangerous. I'm not in any danger here in your place. Maybe the ants running around your kitchen, annoying me, but I won't fall off a ladder here.

Do you know what I did the other day? Now I have time during the day I go for a stroll, I walk until I come to a spot where I feel like stopping and do just that. It's usually the bench in a square or on a main street, like the old folk. All I need to do is feed the pigeons... These strolls don't have any point, I don't make money from them, but I think my head is gradually feeling better. It's like a truce. I don't know whether the peace will be definitive, but when I sit down and enjoy the sun for a while, I take a deep breath and really feel as if

I've returned from the front in some war. Naturally, I can't know what returning from a war is like, but I can imagine. Do you know what must be the worst thing for soldiers? Knowing they're no longer in a war, and taking off their dirty, tattered clothes.

I thought my dress was my own skin yet I still wanted to take it off. Then something strange happened and life took an unexpected turn. I can tell you it was a complete coincidence I happened to stand in front of that hairdresser's. Without the nightshift bonus and overtime I'm harder up than ever and I can't allow myself to throw away my money on this kind of thing, but there was a poster advertising cheap massages. I thought it was rather odd because from outside you could only see hair-dryers and women's heads in silver foil. I went in and made an appointment as if I'd decided to do it some time ago. I thought I'd do my sums later and cut back on other things.

I almost cancelled. I had that same feeling I had when I started coming here, that I knew I needed to come but I told myself, insistently, no, I don't want to go!

And do you know what? I went into that cubicle and immediately felt strangely moved. Yes, really moved. It was the peace and quiet, the slow music, candles and scents. But I was even more moved by the voice of the masseuse when she came in. An older lady with a sad expression. She looked at me the way you do, sir, only she didn't say anything, barely spoke. You know what, she only had to put her hands on me and I felt at one with the world. Well, I don't know if they are the right words, but suddenly in there I didn't feel I needed to resist anything, I didn't have to hide from myself. It was like here, but no words. And each of her caresses made me feel that I was coming home to myself from afar.

I don't know when exactly, but the warmth in her fingers made me start to cry. Do you know why? Well, you know, as her skin rubbed mine, the skin on her fingers, the palms of her hands, her arm over my back, for some peculiar reason, began to remind me of the women in my life, I saw each and every child, young girl and lady I had ever known and saw how I had hated them all. You already knew that in a way I hated them? Especially the simple souls and soft touches, the victims who let themselves be mistreated. The ones who worked night and day in the factory, who let their men beat them up and I realized above all that the women I'd most raged against were those who tolerated their husbands' infidelities. I started to cry, sobbing like a small girl, but the masseuse didn't stop, I reckon she knew exactly what was happening. It was as if touching my skin enabled her to see the stuff I harboured inside myself, all the pain, all that hatred of others and of myself. Do you know what brought the most tears? As I thought back to all those women, in the end one stuck in my mind who wouldn't go away, His wife, the faceless woman, always in the shadow with her two children. I could no longer see her with His eyes, I could only see her with mine and she made me terribly sad. It wasn't her fault, it was His, and I felt very responsible. As responsible as I was for my own suffering. For the first time I recognized her as a victim and felt sorry for her. Then I wept some more because I realized that in a way by betraying her I'd betrayed myself and all the women in the world. For the first time I recognized myself as a victim and felt really sorry for myself.

You, sir, know that I don't like feeling sorry for myself, but perhaps when some things happen, it is a good idea to take that route. When she finished the massage, that woman said very little: what a lot of emotions, right? And put a hand on my shoulder and looked at me.

Later on, naked in front of my mirror, I felt as if I was looking at myself for the first time, whole, refashioned by that woman's hands.

The majority of men I choose are genuine dominators. Over time, you know what people are like in bed long before you find out other things about them. I can guess what a man likes to do there before I know how he likes his coffee. Yes, nobody wants to accept this, but I can tell you that instinct is rarely wrong about such things. Men who like men can detect those who are like themselves, women who like women can distinguish others like themselves in a group of women and I can tell from a set of men the ones who won't be at all gentle in bed. The rough ones, the ones who grab you and make you lose sight of the world, the ones who so dominate you that you don't have to take a single decision. They dominate you, sometimes subtly, by the determined way they control the rhythm of the sex you have with them, but they are often rougher in their intent, more obvious in their wants. You enjoy a good conversation, flirt with them as you would do with any other man, like a couple having fun and everything indicates we will follow the usual steps, sex will begin gradually, that is, casually, tenderly, and then gather steam until he's inside me and staring into my eyes. The first time with many partners is usually friendly like that. But the men I call dominators are only like the others up to the moment of the first kiss. I've known a good few who haven't even respected the first kiss. When you've kissed one of these men, you have burnt up all the fond foreplay, getting to know one another, talking and exploring your body. As you know what they want and they know what you want, they attack your body as if they were already familiar with it, as if there was only one woman's body, as if they were familiar with every body of every woman in the world and were pouring all their rage into yours. Though it's not rage because they aren't angry men, they're not rude or crude or anything of that sort. It's simply that that's what they like and you have chosen each other because that's what you have in common. I was saying how they all generally give you a first kiss that is tenderness itself, slow, light, a gentle touch of the lips, an enjoyable exploration of the texture of the other's skin, their smells and the sticky taste of their saliva. I like that moment of the first kiss and in fact have often thought it's what I have wanted from all men. The moment you close your eyes. Why do I close them? I don't know, but that way I remember the feeling for much longer. Because, despite everything else, there are lips whose touch I like.

Don't get me wrong, it's usually only for a second, it lasts no time at all. Usually it all changes when my partner goes for it and sticks his tongue deep inside, now he's begun to invade me and now it's as if we've both taken off our polite masks and shown ourselves as we want to be. Or is it the reverse? Is it that we take on the role we want to perform? I couldn't tell you, but I am dead sure that when he starts to bite my lips hard, so hard it initially comes as a shock, I now begin to feel closer than ever to the world, my whole body shudders from head to toe and I can forget everything else. They say – I don't – that I turn into a kind of animal and stop being a person. Some take fright but not the dominators. They find confirmation of what they'd suspected I like to do in bed. And they know how to select from all the women around those who want to be dominated. So when they see how I enjoy the bites that almost bring blood, they intensify their bites to the neck, tear at my clothes and move so quickly I don't even have time to think how they're already inside me. They usually spin me round, push me face down and penetrate me from behind. They press on my neck to stop me from moving, hit my face hard against the surface of wherever I happen to be, a pillow in the best of cases, the formica of a kitchen table or tiles on a cold floor. They bite me until they've left an imprint of their teeth marks, but I don't notice the pain until later when I see the shape of their teeth on the skin on my shoulder. Sometimes they pull your hair, alternate that with smashing your face down hard, sometimes slapping your buttocks, something I hardly notice.

But you know what, people are quite wrong about all this. You, sir, must think, like everybody else, that if he is a dominator, I must be submissive, that I long to be dominated. You're wrong, what these men like about me is that you provoke them by refusing to submit, the struggle continues, wrestling as if you don't want what they're doing to you, knowing full well that is *exactly* what you desire. Do you think they'd come after me if I simply offered myself up, lay there quietly, putting up no resistance? No, because that way there'd be no fun, and

I'd have no role to perform. You know what the upshot of all this struggling is, the final outcome, it's simply the peace that descends on two exhausted bodies.

Often when I have come here feeling desperate and told you I needed sex, you, sir, have whispered the word 'love' to me so kindly, like someone letting me into a secret. And, you know, at first I thought it strange because it's a word you only hear in sentimental films when a dim light shines on sloppy kisses in the final scenes, but in fact nobody really knows if they're feeling love or the blast from a moment of hot passion. And don't get me wrong, I'm the sort who is always carried away, but then I snap out of it and tell myself not to be so silly.

Don't you think that love is ridiculous? No, of course, you have to say you don't, but maybe you've not seen what I've seen outside these four walls. And forgive me for saying so but all these issues depend a lot on the kind of luck you've had. If you, sir, believe in love, maybe Lady Luck has been kinder to you. Yes, I know that we determine our own fates, you've often said that. And maybe it's true I've gone for the wrong men all this time, I'm not sure. What can I say? I think it's very reasonable for me not to put any trust in love, right? Hell, you don't understand: I've never seen love, it's like God as far as I'm concerned, nobody can prove it exists. And you have to believe that yours truly wants love more than any other woman you've known.

You'll probably think I'm out of my mind if I say that one way or another I have loved all the men who have passed through me. I tell you, it's true. Not that I love them with a view to marriage or to spending the rest of my life with them, but even when they have disgusted me, I've needed to feel a kind of tenderness or sympathy towards them. Maybe that's why I've fallen out with them, because they couldn't grasp that. But how could they see and treat me tenderly if I wouldn't let them? Yes, I know you must think I'm a real mess and I don't know what I do or don't want, but I can assure you I've been unravelling many of the knots I had inside me talking to you and then talking to myself as if you were listening in. I don't know how you've managed to get inside me the way you have, like a voice that's mine and not mine at the same time.

But you know what? I've not changed so much in some respects. I still feel like that, I still appreciate all the men who are drawn to me, but now there's no way I'll let them stick it inside. Because there are so many ways a man can become part of you, sometimes you don't even need to have sex. You, sir, say there must be a man for me somewhere out there, that in fact there are lots, and now, as I've trusted you rather than myself when I doubt any of this exists, I start to feel impatient. Especially when I think how alone I am, I feel in a terrible rush to find one of these men. I'm so alone, so alone, that one day I might keel over at home and nobody would look for me until I rotted and the neighbours informed the police of the stench, but not because they missed me. No, really, I believe you and keep telling myself I must be prepared to wait for that man of a different ilk. It's just that now I have doubts about everything. In a way, as I'm the one who has attracted the worst imaginable, I don't think I can trust my perceptions. I tell myself that if I've got it wrong over so many years it's not that easy to change my radar and begin to detect the good sort, I mean the guys who will treat me properly. Now there's always something that makes me doubt, that tells me no, no, it can't be this guy because, you know, the way he talks about his mother suggests he's not straightened out his relationship with her, because the way he talks about relationships between men and women you can bet sooner or later he'll want to lock you indoors. Maybe I've become paranoid, but when I'm observing them it's as if I can dig out reams of information about them, much more than they really want to give me. And don't get me wrong, I still feel tempted, but when I think about the fallout, about all the fallout I've experienced I suddenly feel deeply sad. I can't deceive myself like I used to, not for a moment.

I've sometimes started to think I've found him. My heartbeat quickens, races and I get very nervous, but I soon realize he's not the one and all my nerves disappear.

Like who, for example? Well, you know, the guy who is always joking with me in the café where I have *xurros* for breakfast every Saturday morning. I've known him for ages. We get on well after lots of early mornings debating whether the chocolate is too thick or too thin. I like him, you know, always have. He seems made to measure for me, physically, I mean. He sometimes holds my hand and I can feel how it fits mine. I look at him hard and think there's something about him that's not quite right, but I don't know what. Even so, we keep teasing, right? We look at each other, smile at each other, stirring all the time, affectionately. His way of saying hello is often to grab me round the waist and I get goose pimples all over, feel a cold sweat run from head to toe and for a second remember I am alive. I also tease him, and use it to give him two goodbye kisses, for example, to press my lips against his cheeks harder than custom demands. And you can be sure, feeling like I want to kiss him all over, but I suddenly recall that little red light I've had about him all these years and tell myself to stop, no way.

The other day he made it quite clear that he likes me, but did so in a manner that made me very angry. Very.

You know, I'm not the fussy kind, I'm not prickly and don't take offence over trivial things, and though I'm often offended by many of the things men have said to me, I never protested. It hasn't always been like that, has it? Before men weren't so crude in what they said. Well, we were talking about what we'd like to do, holidays in the Caribbean, winning the lottery and giving up work and suddenly he said: do you know what I'd really most like to do? The *only* thing I'd like right now? He looked at me so seriously that I tittered nervously. Obviously I knew what he meant from his question, but he goes on and spells it out: to fuck you. Right now, that's all I want to do.

Can you imagine? And the other women were cackling and crying, like hens in a coop. And I was silent, angry and unable to shed my anger.

So what would I have liked him to say? You'll think I'm being trite, but to be sincere and ditch all my defences, I'd have liked him to say: I like you a lot, I want us to go out together, get to know each other and see if we couldn't build something together. Trite, don't you think?

I'm embarrassed by this dream, particularly because you appear in it, sir, but you once said we are the people in our dreams or at least part of ourselves in there and, in any case, that they're not direct references to the specific individual who appears but only to some of their features. I'll tell you what happened, so you can understand.

I come to your house and tell you I've done one thing and stopped doing another and you congratulate me by jumping for joy: you've finally left all that behind you, you say. Then you hug me and I feel so loved. I could give you a hug, sir, you realize, don't you? But don't get me wrong, I'm not looking for any kind of pleasure or to forget my body, I'd hug you precisely to feel my body more than ever as if it were my own. If I felt your body swaddling me I think I could feel my own and recognize it, make peace and love it. In other words, if you hug me it's very likely I could love myself. That's really what I think when you hug me, I think that, as if that was not only possible but already a reality. I can now recall the precise words I said when I got here: I've left all that behind me. Then you hug me tenderly. As if your body was sexless, as if your body was simply a blanket sheathing mine. When you have this kind of dream, you'd prefer never to wake up, to cling to those sensations for a lifetime. The pity is that it doesn't end particularly well: when you'd just hugged me and I was thinking, look, this man loves you deeply, is very knowledge-able and was about to kiss me, after brushing my hair away from my face. You were coming towards me like they do in old-time films. Music was playing, I think. Yes, music was all around us, and I wanted to kiss you because I felt as if I'd never kissed a man. Then I began to wonder if I'd brushed my teeth or not, that I bet my breath smells, and I sidestepped you so frantically the dream is interrupted right there. How bereft I felt! And all my fault!

I had another very similar dream, but different. More than once recently, especially since I sleep at night now. Know what? Since I've been on sick leave I reckon I work harder asleep than when I worked nights. I sometimes wake up exhausted by a thousand feelings, by stories that disturb me, and I start wondering all kinds of things because I don't understand what they mean. I never used to dream before, I swear I didn't. People say it's just that I don't remember, but that's not true.

In the one dream I had a few nights ago you invited me to your house, which was a kind of museum, and when we are ending the visit you tell me to wait, that you have a surprise for me, that there's still an area we've not seen. You then make me stoop through a low door. There are some caves behind the door that are obviously millions of years old with paintings on the walls. The prehistoric kind. There is a sound of running water. We must wait, you tell me, and a young lad suddenly appears. He looks just like a school friend of mine from years ago, a nice young guy, who suddenly comes over and takes my hand. In fact, he offers me his. And I'm surprised and look at you because I feel rather disconcerted, as if you'd set a trap for me. I look at him and then ask you, incredulously: is he the one? as I point to him. He smiles all the time, waiting for me. But it can't be, I say, it can't be him, but the lad is by my side, wrapping his arms around me. Is it really you? And he smiles and kisses me. So what about the bad breath? He kisses me again and smells me: oh, that's nothing to worry about. I like this smell. We leave the house together and are now at a party with a group of people. Someone asks me how we met, smiling admiringly, as people do admire happy couples. I look at them rather incredulously and excited and we say, in unison, that it's an incredible story. Suddenly, you, sir, are right there standing next to me. And you help me tell that story.

Funny, right? And know what? I think the story we should tell wasn't the one about how he and I met but about all the things that have and haven't happened to me since I've been coming to your house. I don't know, sir, if it's really been worth your while my coming to clean for you, because I have taken up so much of your time. And, obviously, you always say it really has been worthwhile, but it's all extremely odd.

After that dream I look at couples through different eyes. You know, don't you, that when I saw a loving couple I always used to say Agh, even they don't believe it, and I tried to work out how they managed to dupe us all. Not now, now I walk down the street and I see people who do love each other. No, I'm not even ashamed to say as much, right, like some simple soul, but it must be the case, mustn't it, there must be people who love each other, or what sense would all this have? Yes, I know that of necessity we are alone and that nobody can give you what you don't have and that the other person can never make up for your own shortcomings, but I'm sure couples do exist who are good company from day to day, who walk part of the way together. I can never really forgive you for being to blame for turning me into such a trite person. Yes, of course, you will say what you always say, that feelings aren't trite, that love isn't absurd. Well, I can tell you that what you said briefly, almost as an afterthought, must have really got under my skin. I tell you, now I have the time I make every effort not to try to find out which of the men in a relationship is deceiving his wife, but what ways they do in fact love each other. And although this love game isn't a straight road for a lifetime, I guess, I am only just beginning to glimpse that it must be much more pleasant than I ever imagined.

Shall I confess something else? When I now look at couples, talking to each other, taking the dog for a walk, dusting the icing sugar that has got stuck to their partner's lip, putting an arm round their shoulders with that trust that always frightened me, I've not only stopped getting uptight about them, but I think, I'm not sure how, that I'll soon be a member of the same club. There's a frontier between the lonely and the unhappy and those just-about-happy couples and I think I'm now straddling it, with one foot about to break the equilibrium and send me into the other camp. It's stressful, dizzying and exciting – all at the same time.

There *were* good guys around, you know? They've always been there, around me; now, with hindsight, with the peace of mind I've enjoyed ever since I've not touched a man, I can pick them out, though for some odd reason I always avoided them. The good, first-rate guys, the ones I thought weren't for me. Handsome, good-hearted guys and I think some of them even liked me. But I found it hard to believe they liked me... And even now... Well, not anymore, you and I have concluded there is no reason why I shouldn't be worthy of a good man. Except for that bad breath which still stresses me out. There was, for example, a guy in the neighbourhood who wanted to go out with me when I didn't know what that really involved, a guy who was more or less like me whom I called an idiot a number of times and obviously he didn't come back for more. I thought he was laughing at me. Then there was a guy at secondary school who frightened me. But I really don't know if he was one of the good guys because there was something about him I couldn't grasp, that strange feeling men give me and that you say is called intuition. There was another lovely guy at secondary school who always tucked his hair behind his ear and when he smiled he made you think the world was just perfect. I thought it was impossible he could ever consider me. You know, I imagined him with a tall svelte blonde, the thin kind who seem made of air and with waspish waists; however much I'd try to change my body I'd never have managed to be so light. At the time I reckoned that intelligent, handsome, nice men must of necessity prefer easy-going blondes who weighed next to nothing. And don't get me wrong, I wasn't that fat, but I thought that my bones alone weighed more than those ethereal bodies. What a shame I never let myself take the lead, what a shame I always reckoned I only deserved second place, a spot out of the limelight, where I wouldn't get in the way. And you know, I went from there to being a cleaning lady. Now I feel rather sad, I see myself trapped there watching others lead the good life that passed me by. At the time those boys and girls made me feel livid, but the fact was I was the one reining myself in, perhaps to stop myself getting out of control.

I met one of these guys at the factory, don't get me wrong, they're all over the place, I can see that now. A caring guy who took me for a walk in the woods one Saturday night, and kissed me tenderly under the stars and stroked my chin. Naturally, I dropped him as fast as I could, and kept avoiding him until he tired of coming after me. That was a real pity, he was and is what we call a good person and everything would have been so easy with him, I know, he'd have wanted me, would have loved and cherished me.

But you know what? There's no going back. I am sorely tempted at times, you know, especially when I am so alone I don't know what to do with myself. I think I'll ring one of my lovers but I know I never will because I can never go back to all that. Even when I'm slightly tipsy, something buzzes and puts the brake on when a man approaches me. On the other hand, I don't get angry if a man says he likes me and I can see he is the kind I'm better off without who only wants to fuck. I don't get angry, I just say no. No, thank you very much and that's that. It takes a lifetime to learn that, right?

As I was saying, there's no going back, to lovers, or to the good men you might have had a relationship with. They are wasted opportunities. Those encounters happened when they did and when I took the decisions that I took. Afterwards we all changed. I say that because sometimes when I long for one of the few good guys I have known, I start wanting to go and find them in case I could salvage something, but it's best just to keep looking to the future. At least I can hang on to them as part of my past: they weren't just impotent, alcoholic, adulterous, etc, some were good-natured.

But, of course, how could I take notice of them if I was bent on settling for *different*. Crazy, right? Perhaps you understand: I went after guys who were different because they frightened me the most, were enigmatic, unknown quantities, but, as you know, they were all men who frightened me. Not because of what they might do when we were having sex because, as you know, that was never an issue for me. No, what most worried and distressed me in a way I could never control is what happens from the moment our gazes met to when we got into bed, that is, to when we were stripped naked. I never knew what to do with these men in that time, how long it should last, how I should behave, what my role was. That's why I tried to get round that by going to bed with them as soon as I could, and making that interlude as short as possible. I called it passion, being off the leash, being a modern woman, but you know that I was a woman who was shit-scared, who didn't want sex without affection and didn't know how to say as much. Who on earth prepares us for all that? Who teaches you that? Well, nobody, obviously. Can I make a confession? Even now I wouldn't know what to do if I met a man I really liked. The very thought sends me into a spin…

Yes, I know that you tell me I ought to be thinking about what those bad odours in my dreams mean, but I should tell you one thing: today I dreamed I was dying. It was such a lovely prospect.

I got up this morning and a phrase came to me that won't go away: what if this is how it had to be? It first came to me when I was going to the lavatory, still half asleep, it kept echoing around my head, mingling with the flush, the noise from the coffeepot, the light of day until I said it, almost shouted it out, as if I'd just discovered the secret to happiness, what if this is how it had to be?

Of course, you don't understand. You know, sir, ever since you convinced me that one *can* be happy, that there are people who find somebody to live with, to be companions and share hopes together, and not just connect with their sexes, but with minds and emotions, looking after each other, ever since you persuaded me of that, I've always thought to myself but... Can you guess what these buts were about? Well, that I wasn't ready, that it was too soon, that my home wasn't ready to welcome anyone in, and most of all, most of all, that my body wasn't in the right shape. I told myself I should snip a bit off there, smooth that out, clean up that other area, be something else, and, obviously, how could I expect anything to happen when I was thinking like that? I also told myself I had to change my work, my cleaning job, that no good man will want a woman by his side who does that, particularly at night. Well, I think now is the time to change from the night shift, and that's easily done, right? I don't know how yet, but, you know, I've been sleeping so well these last few weeks that I find it hard to imagine going back to daytime sleeping. So I was telling you how I kept repeating to myself that I must change, get my body into good shape, but on the inside as well. I told myself I should be more straightforward, shouldn't turn everything over so much in my head. What man is ever going to want a woman who weeps for days on end and then suddenly laughs, and always for no reason at all? Or a woman who sometimes doesn't clean at all and then cleans like mad, as if the world were coming to an end? Can you imagine the man who could put up with me? But obviously that isn't the right word. It isn't about putting up with me, is it?

Well, you know, today I found it so easy to say I had to be this way and not any other. It's been such a waste, so exhausting trying not to be like this. I only had to utter that phrase to feel released from the weariness I've felt for the last fifteen years, as if I had in fact been trying to change myself for much longer.

I've also been thinking about the bad odour, don't get me wrong, that has a lot to do with that phrase. I first thought the bad odour is my character, it changes so quickly and is so contradictory that sometimes nobody understands me, that can be a very serious handicap if I ever have a man by my side. Then I thought the odour was maybe that collection of men who've passed though me and left their mark, that maybe I have been somehow soiled by them.

But then I've thought about sex and realized that what I

like is filthy and piggish, like wallowing in the mud. And maybe that's not exactly great if you want to find a good man. I used to think I only liked sex with dominators and being dominated, hit, squeezed and bitten because I wanted to forget myself, but now I simply think I like it that way, and that's all there is to it. You don't think this is a kind of illness, do you? The problem is that the men I've been with weren't up for this kind of sex, the best dominators have to be those who love women most, the ones who treat them best. But obviously I don't think it's very easy to find a good man who doesn't reckon that women are inferior, whom you can ask to do this and that to, depending on your fancy, if you get me.

You know, sex is like the theatre. Sometimes, not always, I need sex that's like theatre. Then turns into dreams. In dreams, the things that happen, the people that appear aren't real, aren't flesh and blood. Things mean other things and people either want to be different or are part of yourself. There is a kind of sex where that is exactly what happens. And that's why it can't work if the person I'm playing with is the same as the person he's performing. Do you understand?

Maybe it's not the same for everyone, but I like to be dominated in that game. I've told you that more than once. Not always, of course, some days I feel like peaceful sex without the masks. But when I'm stressed out, if I'm working a lot, if I'm tired, the only thing I crave is for a man to come and help me forget the world. I used to think I needed to forget my own body because I hated it, and that really disgusted me. But not anymore, now what I want is to forget the world precisely to rediscover myself.

Yes, it's that complicated, I want a man whom I love and who loves me, and I want him to tie me up, blindfold me, bite my back and leave me with lots of half-moon bites and sink his fingers into the cavities in the back of my neck, right? Where my head joins my body. I want his fingers to press me hard and deep into the mattress. I'd resist, naturally, as if I didn't want all that, but, as he knows me well, he wouldn't stop. Then I'd get him to turn me over and he'd grab my neck as I'm struggling to breathe, as if he wants to strangle me. You must see how important it is to do all this with a man who doesn't in fact really want to hurt you. Giving me pleasure is a sacrifice he makes for me, good dominators don't usually derive pleasure from hurting and feel pleasure when they see the woman experiencing pleasure when she is feeling pain. They are quite different things. Do you realize I've only just understood that? In the same way that dominators who want to dominate can't be people who mistreat you in real life, dominated women can't be victims or submissive because otherwise they wouldn't be engaged in a game, it would be for real.

It is complicated, isn't it? Yes, I know, you, sir, tell me it is logical enough, but what man will ever understand that? Isn't that asking too much? You always say it isn't, that I must simply let myself believe that they do exist.

For the moment I've just one other thing I can tell you: I think the bad odour in dreams is a thing of the past. Today I had another dream in which I was with a man who was going to kiss me, when I stopped myself because of the odour. However, this time, still in my dreams, when the scene froze

I said angrily: not again? It can't be true, I'm fed up with this, it has to stop. And do you know what I did? I went to a specialist, an ear, nose and throat specialist, and turning back into myself, as if watching a re-play of the scene, I sent myself this message: that's the last time that will happen, don't you worry.

You say, sir, that you write happy endings and I'd not believed you to this point. Of course, they always say they are too easy and bland, trite and idealistic, but maybe that's because they only show us part of these happy endings. And because there are only two hours to tell the story in a film that often means we only see half the story. I've been turning real life into ninety-minute films but now I think I can live the whole lot. Agh, you see how you make me spout such clichés?

If I'd known it was so easy I'd not have taken so long, but maybe I had to learn what I've learned in order to make it so easy. It's not a matter of luck, but, as you were saying, things can be so simple.

For days I've been going for very early morning walks. After living in reverse for so long, you don't know how happy I feel getting up early and going out for a walk when the air is fresh and the day is just kicking off. I sometimes run, when I feel my body's disappearing and I can't feel it, I run until I can't run anymore. Well, you know, I always take the same route, every day, when I'm still savouring my dreams.

The other day I had such a lovely dream. Sorry to be so boring but I've never had such bright, lucid dreams. A man came to call for me and we both mounted a giant bird with feathers of a thousand hues, dizzying, I tell you. But I held on tight and wasn't scared. Do you know what I found at the bottom of a valley the bird suddenly plunged into? I was there in a pale blue dress I had when I was a little girl waving giant worms that were writhing round my fingers. The girl swung round and smiled at us. I was thinking about that when somebody suddenly stopped me in the middle of the path on the outskirts of town, where the scents of the earth and plants were really pungent. Sorry, I think you've dropped something. And it was a man I see every morning, who runs in the other direction and he was pointing at my keys on the ground. I'd not heard them fall I'd been so absorbed in remembering my dream. He stooped and returned them to me and I stared at him, still at a loss.

You, sir, always say that I'll know him when I see him, sorry to say this, but you sound rather like a witch when you say these things. I told you I didn't trust my radar, that I could no longer trust my intuition that had misled me for so long, but you insisted that intuition had always been there and working well, but I'd concealed it so as not to protect myself, and that this was a defect of my own making.

Well, you know, you must have been right, because when I saw that young man I told myself this is the one, I don't know why, but he looked like a good person. I got so agitated, so wanted to run that I said thank you and rushed off as if a fire was raging. Then I forgot the whole business, thought it was another of my flash-in-the-pans that lead nowhere, but the day after, when we passed each other, he smiled. You know what? You won't believe this. We were both running and suddenly, when we were level, we stopped dead and stared, saying nothing, observing each other, testing the terrain. Suddenly I wasn't scared, wasn't in a rush and didn't avoid his gaze. I thought this is too serious, I should give him a good look-over to have the necessary to decide if I liked him enough. What a sight we must have been transfixed there, like animals meeting and sniffing, not saying a word. I scratched an eyebrow with a couple of fingers while I thought and glanced at the ground for a moment, and when our eyes met again, would you believe it, at the same time we both asked: how about meeting up? And then, of course, we couldn't stop laughing. We introduced ourselves, shook hands as if we'd done a deal and agreed to meet for dinner the following day in a restaurant in the city centre. If you like, after that we can go to the cinema or for a drink. Let's decide then, I replied, and ran off, suddenly grinning broadly, a grin I'd been trying to stifle for some time.

We had supper and know what? I'm no longer afraid. I listen to myself and listen to see if the voice lurking behind my voice is alerting me to danger. For the moment it isn't. I can hear his desire and the way he looks at parts of my body when he's speaking to me, though he makes every effort to pretend he's not. Do you know why I don't get angry? Because I no longer find it odd that he likes my body, I like it and like it even more now that it's accompanied by that little word 'my'. And I like him and I like his body and I don't feel disgust if I imagine I will be seeing it naked. But I'm biding my time. I'm in no rush. I know this is how it ought to be, that we'll gradually get to know each other and that sex will come one day after love and sex will be wonderful, do you know why? Because it will be sex that is human and tender.